BEFORE
HIS TIME

JOHN DAVID FENNER

THE SPIRIT WARRIOR

BEFORE
HIS TIME

TATE PUBLISHING
AND ENTERPRISES, LLC

Published by Tate Publishing & Enterprises, LLC
127 E. Trade Center Terrace | Mustang, Oklahoma 73064 USA
1.888.361.9473 | www.tatepublishing.com

Tate Publishing is committed to excellence in the publishing industry. The company reflects the philosophy established by the founders, based on Psalm 68:11, *"The Lord gave the word and great was the company of those who published it."*

Published in the United States of America

ISBN: 978-1-62510-098-6
1. Fiction / Science Fiction / Time Travel
2. Fiction / Native American & Aboriginal
13.07.17

DEDICATION

This book is for all American Indians, Native Americans, or First Immigrants and for the nicest person I know, my beautiful wife, Tatiana Kotovich Fenner.

ARRIVAL IN A STRANGE LAND

The sun felt warm on his face as he lay there with his eyes closed. He could feel the breeze wafting over his naked body and smell the freshness of the grass in which he reposed. He was very relaxed and rested, his mind drifting aimlessly, one random thought to another... Suddenly this relaxation ended, his thoughts focused and his eyes snapped open, squinting against the brightness of the overhead sun. Where was he, and what was he doing here?

He sat up and looked around. He was lying on a patch of tall, green grass on a slope. His eyes confronted a scene of a gently rolling plain covered with waving knee high grasses, stretching far as his eyes could see. Looking down at himself, he could see that he was entirely naked, not a stitch on!

He had no recollection of arriving at this place and had no idea where he was. His last memory was of Bob, his dentist, intoning the relaxing, hypnotic phrases, to prepare him for minor dental work. His tongue sought the chip in his incisor and found it filled in with dental material, the edges still sharp. His memory of the dentist visit was correct, but how and why was he on this lonely hillside...and naked?

Bryan rolled to his knees and then stood up and looked around some more. The elevated height did nothing to improve his knowledge of where he was. He could see nothing more than he had while down in the grass, just more of the hillside on which he had found himself. The ground under his bare feet felt soft with the thatch of older grasses, but he could feel the firmness of the earth underneath. His hands automatically brushed grass and dirt off his bare backside before he strode up the gentle slope toward the crest of the hill.

His loping stride was easy, his long, well-muscled legs making short work of the climb. He stood on the hilltop and surveyed the surroundings, a moderately tall, muscular, young man with ruddy skin and longish, dark hair. He was almost devoid of body hair, other than at his groin, and his body showed the results of hard training in the gym and karate dojo.

From this vantage point, Bryan could see a seemingly endless horizon, a sun-swept, rolling grassland stretching in all directions. The sun was nearly overhead, but instinct told him that he had been lying on a westerly slope. Facing what he felt to be west, he could see a darker patch of green in the distance, which could be treetops in a draw or creek bed. He stifled his rising concern with his unfamiliar surroundings and situation and gave in to curiosity. He set out in that direction with an easy swinging stride, after checking around to see if he had in fact come to this spot with nothing but his birthday suit. His feet were well calloused from years of training and competing barefoot on hardwood or concrete floors, so he felt only mild discomfort when his foot came down on clods or pebbles in the thatch underfoot.

As he made his way toward the distant trees, he tried to make sense of his situation. He had gone to the dentist, Bob Broome, who was also one of the students in Bryan's karate dojo, to repair a chip in a tooth. Bob used hypnosis as an anesthetic in minor work, as he explained to Bryan, preferring not to leave the patient numb for hours afterward. Bryan's last recollection was of being fully reclined in the chair, sinking into sleeplike relaxation, hearing Bob's reassuring voice from behind him.

"You will feel nothing as you sleep... No noises will disturb you... You will be relaxed and peaceful..."

His tongue sought his tooth again and was reassured in finding that the repair work had indeed been done. But nothing else made sense.

Bryan McKay, at least until a few moments ago, resided in Jasper, a small farming oriented city in the mountains of south-central Pennsylvania, just west of the Pennsylvania Dutch country. Bryan taught history in one of two local High Schools, a career he had selected more from necessity than from choice. He also taught Goju Kenpo, a karate style from Okinawa, in a local dojo on three nights a week.

As a child, Bryan had been thrilled by his mother's stories of visiting her grandfather on the Seneca reservation in Salamanca, New York. He was proud of his American

Indian heritage and read everything he could about the original Americans. His play often involved stalking in the forested hills near town, practicing the woodcraft he had read about. He became an accomplished woodsman at an early age.

Bryan had gotten involved in the martial arts when, as a twelve year old, he had attended a Bruce Lee movie with some friends in which the hero used karate techniques to overcome adversaries. The movements of Master Lee had mesmerized him. He couldn't even remember the movie, only the ease with which the slight Eurasian handled the villains.

It had taken him a week of working on his mother before she had enrolled him in a local karate dojo, accompanied by the admonition that his grades in school had better not suffer or no more karate!

He proved an enthusiastic student, progressing from the beginning white obi to yellow, orange, blue, green, purple, and brown. While still in high school, Bryan attained the rank of *shodan* or first-degree black belt. During this period, instead of suffering, his grades in school improved because of the self-discipline he garnered from his training. He still found time for other school and social activities, but he always regularly attended the karate training classes.

As he strode across the grassy terrain, Bryan took note of his surroundings, as much from a response to his training as for any other reason. After college, which he had attended with the aid of an Army ROTC scholarship, he had served much of his four-year military obligation as a platoon leader in the Airborne Rangers, where he had been subjected to intense survival training, so he now took note of edible roots and plants, like wild onions and others, which he identified amongst the grasses. He might not thrive, but he certainly would not starve. He also knew that anywhere there was edible vegetation, there were usually animals that fed on it, and they would be a critical source of protein and fat that his body would need to supplement the vegetable carbohydrates.

His initial panic at finding himself in this strange situation was now totally suppressed as he focused on survival, the natural response to all his training.

He arrived at a hillock overlooking the copse of trees after about half an hour of trekking. The trees appeared to be a type creek-willow, indicating a water source. He made his way down the slope and among the trees found a creek. The water was clear and clean, flowing smoothly over rocks and pebbles. It tasted good, and he drank his fill.

His thirst satisfied, he began to consider his situation. The source of the stream was probably far to the north, maybe in a lake or from the convolution of smaller streams that arose in the mountains. The line of trees bordered the stream that meandered through the low-lying area of the rolling countryside. In the sandy soil deposited by the stream along a curve in its course, he saw the tracks of cloven-hoofed animals, possibly antelopes or deer. Badger-like tracks abounded along this bank, as well as signs of partridge-sized birds.

Bryan set about preparing himself for survival. First, he plaited a strong rope from willow bark, which he softened by kneading it between smooth rocks, and long grasses from the hillside. When he had about four feet of it, he wound it about his waist as a belt.

His next step was hunting implements. He searched along the bank until he found a deadfall, from which he broke a well-seasoned, forked branch. With a sharp stone, he stripped the remaining bark and cut off the smaller branch of the fork, leaving a two-foot stick, bent near the middle at a thirty-degree angle, a large knot at the bend. With the sharp stone, he scrapped the sides smooth. He had fashioned a primitive hunter's throwing stick, good for bringing down small game.

He practiced throwing the stick at a clump of grass on the stream bank and found that he had nearly gotten the balance right. After a little while of throwing, scraping, and modifying the device, he had a weapon which he felt would suffice. Continued practice developed his eye until he was quite proficient, striking the targets often.

The sharp-edged stone had worked effectively as a hand axe, so he tied it in the loose ends of the belt, where it would ride without causing him any discomfort. He then found a piece of dead wood about six feet long, reasonably straight and about an inch and a half in diameter. This would be a walking stick and also serve as a defensive weapon, a Bo, widely used in Okinawa and Chinese martial arts.

He figured that if he followed the course of the stream he would not want for water, and maybe find some game, possibly even other people. He selected to go north, toward the source, for no particular reason. Going north he might find a lake in which there would be fish or fowl and other game. South, the stream might join others and broaden, making crossing more dangerous. North it was. He stuck the throwing stick through his belt, took up his Bo, and started out.

THE OLD ONE

The old man sat in the darkness, eyes closed, rocking slowly back and forth. He was coming out of the trance induced by his ingesting of the mind-freeing plant, the one he had learned about from his mentor so many years ago. His body felt light as if he had lost substance while mind traveling, but he knew that was not really the case, just the illusion of the drug. He began to be more aware of his surroundings—the soft robe beneath him, the red glow from the few coals remaining from his fire, the dim light peeking around the smoke-hole flap, and the muted sounds of the village penetrating his consciousness.

The old man felt refreshed now but knew that later, he would be exhausted from his efforts in the netherworld of mind-traveling, but he was pleased because this time he had made contact, this time he had started something which could save his people, this time the spirits had answered him...

Legend told of the warrior spirit who had come to The People in a time of need many, many seasons ago, before they had lost the corn, before they had fled their oppressors by the great waters to the northeast, before they had come to this great plain and made their home, before they had become nomads following the great herds on which their survival depended... Before all this, during a time of great peril, their shaman had called upon the spirits to send them a great warrior, one to show them the way to fight their enemies, to lead the warriors of The People against those who would drive them from their villages, their fields of corn, their home for as long as their history could recall. The spirits had responded, and a great warrior had come amongst them and taught The People the ways of war.

They had prevailed at first, pushing their enemies back and holding them at bay for generations, but the lessons of the great warrior had been lost through neglect during the period of peace brought about by their martial skills, and The People had been uprooted from their homeland. Their leaders had guided them away from the great waters, to the southwest, onto the Great Plains. They moved rapidly, and the pursuit was short-lived for the invader had only wanted their rich land.

Now, many generations later, a new oppressor had come. Once again, The People needed a savior to train them and to lead them into battle, and the old man, as shaman, had been calling upon all his powers to make contact with the spirits to send them this great warrior once again. For moons, he had been trying but to no avail, exhausting himself and taxing the limits of his magic he had learned from his mentor. Recently, he had fasted and asked for a vision to guide him, offering anything the spirits demanded as exchange, even his own life for the safety of his people... He had received his vision, but the cost was unclear. The People needed to again learn the arts of war...so they could live in peace.

He sat there, feeling the weariness descending upon his aged body. He would have to eat something to regain some strength and then report the latest developments to the chief. With an effort, he rolled forward and pushed himself up off the ground and stood, his joints creaking from their long inactivity. He made his way to the entrance and pushed the hide flap open and ducked through the doorway. It was nearing dusk, and cooking fires were glowing all over the camp. Overhead, the sky was dark blue, and brighter stars were beginning to gleam. His eyes sought out the sky sign of the warrior just beginning to show on the eastern horizon. Tonight the group of stars seemed brighter somehow, a brightness of promise, of a legend coming alive again after an absence of thousands and thousands of such nights.

The old shaman made his way toward the center of the village where stood the lodge of the clan leader. At the door flap, he scratched on the tepee wall with his fingers and awaited the invitation to enter.

The chief, an older man, but far younger than the shaman, was seated across the small fire from the entrance. He bade the old man to be seated on his right, the place of honor. Almost immediately, a horn bowl of stew was placed in his hands and another given to the chief by his senior wife. They ate with polite noisiness, a comfortable belch after the bowls were emptied.

The chief pulled his pipe from its pouch, tamped some tobacco into the bowl, and lit it with a coal from the fire, which he fished out with a pair of sticks. The heady aroma of the precious leaf soon filled the air. The chief offered to the heavens and the four points of the compass, and he then proffered the glowing pipe to the holy man and waited patiently while the older man performed the same ritual. When he was done, the old man cleared his throat and began.

NOT ALONE

For the remainder of the day, he followed the wandering stream in a northerly direction, pausing occasionally to check out the surroundings and scout for edibles. The terrain changed somewhat as the elevation rose, the hillsides becoming steeper and sporting more trees, first in small clumps, then in larger copses of birch, alder, and some evergreen.

As the sun began to drop to the western horizon, Bryan began to seek out something to eat. He had spotted some small game, rabbits and a few birds that looked to be some type of partridge or prairie chicken, but he had not stopped to hunt. But now, the rumbling in his stomach signaled a need to eat. In a copse of trees on the hillside, he found wild leeks, an onion-like tuber, growing in profusion, and he gathered an armful, carrying them down to the stream bank. He gathered some dry wood and grass and set about building a fire in a ring of rocks he set up in the sandy soil.

On a flat piece of dead wood, he bored a hole with a sharp stone. He then selected a straight stick on which he had ground a point by working it on one of the stones. With a smaller, flat piece of wood as a top, his grass rope looped across another stick, forming a bow, he put some dried moss in the hole on the base board, put the point of the stick into it, looped the rope around it, and placed the top into the hole in the top piece. By moving the bow back and forth, he rotated the fire stick and created frictional heat in the hole in the baseboard, igniting the dried moss. When there was a glowing coal, he added more moss and continued to ply the bow until there was a finger of flame. Carefully, he added some more moss and then transferred the flame to his tinder, which began to burn immediately. Shortly, Bryan had a good fire going, the warmth of which felt good in the evening chill on his bare skin.

A large piece of willow bark formed a crude bowl into which he added water and the leeks. Making sure to keep the fire below the level of the water in the bark bowl by resting the sides on more piled rocks, he waited while the soup began to simmer, then boil. After about thirty minutes, he had a bowl of piping hot leek soup.

If only I had a little salt, he mused, *it would be a meal fit for a king.* The flavor of the soup was strong, but it tasted good and satisfied his appetite, stopping the stomach rumblings for a while.

He located a cut under the stream bank where spring floods had washed out a small niche, and he dragged some dead leaves and grass into it, forming a nest, then collapsed into it, burrowing into his bed and dragging more leaves over him. He hoped that it wouldn't get too cold because he had no other cover, but the leaves and grass should help keep his body warmth in his nest.

He awoke just before dawn, cold and stiff in every joint. He groaned audibly as he crawled from his den and stretched and twisted himself, trying to ease his discomfort. After relieving himself, he began to do a "daily dozen" of stretching exercises to warm his muscles and loosen his joints. This completed, he felt immensely better and set about to quiet the rumbling in his gut. He knew that the few plants he would find would not satisfy his need, so he gathered up his meager possessions and began to work his way up the stream, watchful for any signs of game.

Bryan's response to the situation was a product of his intensive training, and though he was puzzled and concerned about where and why he was in this place, his survival was the most immediate need. Later, when his basic needs were satisfied—food, shelter, and protection against the elements—he would attack that problem. His common sense told him that there was nothing he could do until he had achieved some level of comfort and safety. The immediate problem was he didn't know what each of these entailed, and although the terrain and flora did not appear alien to his experience and training so far, he had no idea where he was. He had accepted the fact that he was far from home, but how far and in which direction? He was not a believer in the supernatural, nor was he enough of a scientist to explain the phenomenon of his being in this place.

During his brief time here, he gradually became aware of the absence of any signs of civilization as he knew it. There had been no aircraft passing overhead, nor at night, had he seen the horizon glow from cities or towns. The stars in the night sky had appeared undiminished by manmade interference.

Bryan found a few more of the edible tubers and chewed them raw as he cast about for tracks along the stream banks, looking particularly for small game—birds, rabbits, or squirrels—since his limited weaponry afforded him no opportunity for larger game. Plus, he had no way of storing any excess meat at present.

The trees lining the creek were willows, which didn't bear any fruit that would attract squirrels or other tree dwellers. His examination of the branches overhead confirmed this, but his eyes glimpsed tracks on a sandbar on the creek edge. Closer examination showed them to be those of the partridge-sized birds. He followed these toward a brushy hillside, toward a stand of trees, moving slowly, pausing often. He was rewarded on one of his pauses by a loud whirring of wings as several prairie grouse rose from the grass almost underfoot. He was initially startled even though he had been expecting this, and he nearly missed his chance. His reflexes and practice with the throwing stick proved out as one of the birds dropped from his rapid fling. He ran quickly to the stunned bird and smothered it with his hands before it could recover and escape. A quick twist of the head and he was ready to clean and dress the bird.

Back at the stream with the bird, he gathered up some dry twigs, sticks, and branches from a tangle left by a spring flood surge. Selecting a straight, hard stick about two feet long and a flat piece of driftwood, he set about making another fire drill. Shortly, he had another fire going, and the spitted bird was suspended to one side on green willow branches sunk into the soft ground. Shortly, the aroma of cooking poultry began to fill the air, and Bryan found himself salivating. When it was crisp and dripping, he removed it from the fire and began to enjoy his first real meal in this place. *All I need*, he thought, *is a little seasoning and a good white wine, maybe a Moselle.* He made short work of the delicious bird and then washed his hands at the stream, using sand as a cleanser.

Feeling very satisfied and confident of his ability to cope with his situation, he drank his fill and continued his journey, now at a faster pace.

As the sun passed its zenith and began to sink toward the horizon, Bryan was just topping a rise when a sight made him freeze in his tracks, then sink slowly to the ground until he was out of sight. On the downside slope was a small herd of antelope that he recognized as pronghorn, indigenous to the American prairie. The animals were not alarmed and were browsing. Bryan eased his head up until he could see the beasts and looked them over. One of them, a large ram, was trailing the group as it moved across the slope, browsing in the knee-high grass, and he moved haltingly. Soon, he lay down rather heavily. The herd continued to graze, moving away from him, but the ram didn't rise and follow, just lay there, his sides heaving as if he had just run a great distance and was catching his wind.

Bryan eased down the slope toward the reclining antelope, his Bo at the ready to strike or throw at the ram's legs when he rose to escape. When he was a dozen yards away, the ram struggled to rise, but before he could, Bryan was upon him with the staff, striking a mighty blow to the animal's neck. There was an audible crack, and the beast slumped to the ground and lay still.

Pleased with himself, Bryan surveyed the motionless animal while he figured out how to dress him out. He took a foreleg to roll the ram over on his back, and as the animal turned, he was stunned to see the broken end of a wooden shaft protruding from behind the animal's shoulder.

He was transfixed... The antelope had been shot by another hunter and not long ago. That was why the animal had not been more alert and was easy prey for his stalk and attack. Where was this other hunter? He cast his eyes in every direction but saw nothing except the other antelope, which had stopped several hundred yards away, on the opposite slope and was looking back curiously. He looked back at his quarry. There was about six inches of wooden shaft, broken at the end, emerging from an area just behind the shoulder, probably penetrating the heart/lung area. The wound would have been fatal to the animal in a matter of hours, maybe less, if Bryan hadn't luckily stumbled upon him.

He bent and began to try and work the arrow from the wound, figuring to use the arrowhead as a substitute knife and field dress the ram. He worked at the shaft and finally was able to pull it free from the wound, a gush of blood following its withdrawal. The point was long, narrow, fluted, and appeared to be made of flint! It was attached to the shaft by a tight wrapping of very thin leather. He had a tool, but who had fashioned it, and where was he? Someone who really wanted to get primitive in their hunting... Or was Bryan somewhere other than the good old US of A!

THE PEOPLE

"I have seen the face of the great warrior who will come to us," began the shaman. "He does not appear to be of The People, being much taller and lighter of skin, but he has the look of an eagle."

The chief reflected for a moment, then asked, "When will he come among us?"

"The Spirit Warrior has not told me this, but his pull was very strong, and I think he will be coming soon."

"It cannot be too soon," replied the chief. "The Omaha and Iowa will be sending out raiding parties before the snow flies, and they could locate our camp. I may order the move to our wintering grounds rather than risk an attack by our enemies."

"I will rest a while, then enter the Spirit World again. I will seek out the Spirit Warrior and ask him."

The old man struggled to his feet and left the lodge, making his way back to his own teepee. The camp of twenty lodges was becoming quiet with everyone settling in for the evening meal and only a few dogs barked sporadically. When he got to his lodge, he found that his younger daughter had prepared a thin stew from dried meat, wild onion and tubers, flavored with herbs. He was almost too tired to eat, but he knew he needed his strength, so he slowly ate a bowl with a horn spoon before retiring to his couch of furs to rest before the next ordeal.

As he reclined, his eyes traveled over the painted hides that adorned the walls of his lodge. On them were recorded the history of The People as had been passed down from generation to generation. The paintings had been rendered by the many shamans before him and showed a wide variety of painting skills. They traced the origins of the tribe from their creation by The Earth Mother to their present nomadic life. His contribution was a work in progress, and the hide of which was stretched on an easel against the skin wall of the tepee.

Once a numerous tribe of farmers living in permanent villages on the shores of the Great Lake to the northeast, The People had been pushed from their homelands by tribes more skilled in the art of war and forced to live a nomadic life on the prairies, following the game herds. After they "lost the corn," they had splintered into small clan or family groups of ten to twenty lodges and scattered across the plains, coming together only once a year at a great summer gathering. This made them vulnerable but enabled them to hunt and gather food over a broader area, so they didn't deplete the resources. These and other events were recorded on the lodge hangings.

The Gathering gave them an opportunity to visit relatives, form alliances, exchange goods and information on hunting and food gathering. The warriors engaged in athletic contests and competition involving their hunting skills—archery and spear throwing. It also gave the young men the chance to meet marriageable girls from other family groups.

During the last gathering, the elders gathered and discussed the growing number of attacks from more aggressive tribes to the east. After years of relative peace and harmony, their enemies were again raiding for food, weapons, and women. They recalled that once, many, many summers past, the most senior shaman had been able to visit the Spirit World and plead for assistance. This had come in the form of a Spirit Warrior who had taught the young men the arts of war. The People were now similarly oppressed, and the elders had asked the Sachem to attempt to call up the Spirit Warrior of their past.

It was late evening, and the camp had quieted for the night when the old Sachem rose from his sleeping furs to begin the ritual for entry into the Spirit World. He gathered the necessary elements from his parfleche and his medicine bag, totem, and the cactus buttons that freed his mind. He made a potion with the water his daughter had left in the bark bowl near the fire and drank it down. He leaned against his bone and hide backrest and waited for the drug to take effect.

It wasn't long before he entered the Spirit World. As on his previous visits, he saw a kaleidoscope of colors and unclear images dancing behind his eyelids. He was dizzy and pressed against the backrest to calm the nausea that rose in his throat. Soon, his vision cleared, and he saw clearly the strong-looking young man. He was naked except for a grass rope around his waist and some primitive-looking hunting tools. The Spirit Warrior appeared to be following a small stream that the old man didn't recognize, except that the terrain appeared similar to an area several days travel to the east.

The shaman called to the Spirit Warrior with his mind, asking him to come to the people, to help in their time of great need. The young man paused as if hearing the call, then looked directly into the old man's eyes.

PREPARING FOR SURVIVAL

Bryan examined the flint blade of the arrow. It appeared well made and quite sharp. The remaining shaft would make a good handle when wrapped with something to give better purchase and grip. A piece of his grass rope would do until he had something better, so he sliced some off using the flint blade and tightly wrapped the shaft. He tried his new knife and found it fit his hand well and would be serviceable.

Rolling the antelope buck on its back and propping it there with a large rock on either side, he proceeded to dress out the beast. Having done this a number of times with white-tailed deer in his home Pennsylvania woods, he found the antelope quite similar, and the task was fairly easy. He removed the heart and liver and set them aside for immediate cooking. He discarded the other viscera; then as carefully as possible, he removed the skin. His new knife worked quite well, and he was pleased.

Bryan cut up the carcass into manageable sized pieces, rolled them in the hide, and carried them into the nearby trees. He gathered a sizeable amount of dried wood from deadfalls and used his fire drill to start a blaze. While waiting for the fire to die down to cooking coals, he located a number of forked and long, straight green tree branches to be used to cook his meat. With the flint knife, he cut the liver and heart into strips that he suspended over the fire on green branches. He then began to butcher the large cuts of meat, cutting them into long strips, which he placed on a drying rack made from more of the green tree limbs. Using four-forked branches for the corner uprights, then placing four straight branches between made his rack. On this frame, he placed cross members of more green branches creating a rack suspended high enough above the fire so as not to burn but close enough that the heat would dry, or jerk, the meat. It was the only method he had of preserving the antelope.

The heart and liver strips were soon cooked, and he dined while the other meat smoked and dried. He then gathered more firewood, knowing that it was going to take hours to finish his jerky. He wished he knew more about what herbs that might be growing nearby so he could flavor the jerky, but nourishment was the important factor, not taste...though he did enjoy the animal's liver a lot.

Throughout the day that it took to make the jerky, Bryan thought about his situation. He was still baffled about where he was and how he got there. When he had first awakened in this place, he thought he might be the victim of a prank by his student-dentist, Bob Broome, and others from the karate dojo. He quickly dismissed this idea because he was obviously a long way from south-central Pennsylvania. The antelope were animals of the western plains, but how did he get here, and just where was "here?" He had no clothes, no watch, no pocket change or pocketknife... He had nothing but the suit he was born in. How did all this happen? His survival training had kicked in immediately, a reaction to his intense training in the rangers, but now as he waited for the meat to cure, he had time to think about the fix he was in. His organized mind had already established priorities—food, clothing, and shelter—and two of those were nearly satisfied.

He set about scraping the antelope hide of any remaining meat or fat, working the hide so it would be as soft as he could get it without tanning. It would serve as clothing and as a blanket at night. Brian recalled from his survival training that tannin could be used as a preservative for animal skins. He also recalled that tannin is found in a number of plants, including bark and leaves of trees, most notably the oaks. The trees around him weren't oak, but maybe willows or cottonwoods, he wasn't sure. Thinking he had nothing to lose, he gathered bark from several trees, made a large, shallow pit on the creek bank, which began to seep and puddle with water. To speed the process, he scooped water from the stream with his hands, splashing it into the rapidly filling pit. He placed chunks of bark in the pit and was pleased to see an immediate coloring of the water. He immersed the hide in the puddle, placed more bark on top, and weighted it all down with stones. He would have to keep an eye on the puddle to make sure it was kept full of water.

All the while he worked, Bryan's mind kept flashing back to his situation. By keeping busy with survival, he hadn't had the time to analyze it any more than to realize he was somewhere in a wilderness and must assure his survival before trying to figure out how to get back home, wherever that was from here. Now, while waiting for his meat and hide to cure, he had time to think.

It seemed to him that the first thing to figure out was where he was. The flint arrowhead was part of the puzzle, but it did indicate he wasn't totally alone, wherever he was. The flora and fauna indicated he was somewhere in the central plains area of North America. So far, there had been no indications of civilization, such as aircraft passing overhead or human debris often found around streambeds. There had been no signs of vehicle tracks. How long had he been under hypnosis to be transported to his present location? Who transported him and why? The more he thought about it, the less he knew, but at least, his interests and training had prepared him for this... In fact, if he could find the answers to a few of his questions, he might actually enjoy this experience!

Bryan Andrew MacKay had been born in south-central Pennsylvania thirty-two years before. His parents were pleasant middle-class people who were both born and raised in the same area and were high school sweethearts who married while both were attending the nearby State Teachers College. Bryan's dad was a professor at this same college while his mother taught second grade at Jasper Elementary. Two years after Bryan, they had a second child, another son, Jason. Both children were raised with affection and attention.

Even as a youngster, Bryan had felt a little out of sync with his contemporaries. An early reader, he devoured books of all sorts, his favorites being tales of early America, medieval times and knights in armor, and sagas of warriors of every stripe. He also loved the outdoors and spent many days roaming the wooded hillsides of his home area. He often fantasized about being an explorer, an adventurer on a quest, or, influenced by his mother's stories of her Iroquoian heritage, he was an Indian warrior bent on raiding a hostile village.

Bryan loved physical challenges and threw himself into every available sport, both in school and in pickup games in the neighborhood. He was well coordinated, quick, and competitive.

While in his early teens, there was an experience that changed his life. He was coaxed into attending a Saturday matinee at a local theater by a couple of friends. He had planned on playing baseball, but they were persuasive and off they went on their bikes to the movies. After a few cartoons and a couple of short comedies, the feature started. It was a martial arts film featuring Bruce Lee. The slight Eurasian kung fu stylist and the ease with which he handled opposition immediately mesmerized Bryan. The point of the story was lost along the way, something about a Buddhist monk, trained in martial discipline who used his skills to right wrongs, knock out bad guys, and rescue damsels in distress. But Bryan was rapt about Master Lee's skills.

Back at home, he searched the telephone directory and discovered that there was, in fact, a martial arts school in Jasper, Pennsylvania. The school featured an Okinawa style of karate called Goju Kenpo, which hailed itself in the display AD as "The Warrior's Way."

Bryan's parents, though not indulgent, agreed to allow him to audit one of the classes at the dojo and, if the costs weren't great, would allow him to attend classes with a couple of stipulations, being his grades would not suffer and he would not neglect his household chores.

A very excited young man entered the dojo the next evening at six o'clock. The dojo was located in a strip mall next to a convenience store. The view to the inside was partially obscured by a semitranslucent sign that proclaimed Karate across the storefront windows. There was a small entrance foyer with a desk and telephone and no one in attendance, but Bryan could see through the glass interior door that there was one large room with no furnishing except a few folding chairs along one wall. A large boxing type heavy bag was suspended from the ceiling in one corner, but other than that, there was no visible equipment. The far wall was mirrored. He entered and took a seat on one of the folding chairs.

There were a number of students of both sexes dressed in white canvas pants and tops, tied at the waist with belts of assorted colors, ranging from white through yellow, orange, blue, green, purple, brown, and black. The students were stretching and practicing kicks, blocks, and punches. A few were kicking the heavy bag.

Bryan was later to learn that ranking in the system went from white, a beginner, to brown, an advanced student, in ten steps or *que*. Then, there were ten degrees of black belts, with sixth degree and above being considered a master of the system. Other martial arts systems have similar rankings, though not always designated by the same colors. The belt colors start with white then get darker with increased rank. The original belts used were all of heavy white canvas. Early karate practitioners had a superstition that if they washed their belts they would lose their power; thus, the belts grew progressively darker as their skills advanced.

Over the years, Bryan always the curious student studied the histories of several martial arts systems. Karate, he had read, had origins in India where Monks practiced the moves as a form of physical discipline. Shaolin Buddhist Monks in China picked it up and transformed it further, developing an effective self-defense system. In Korea and Okinawa, "hard styles" of karate were developed, featuring hard blocks, breaking of boards, and direct moves rather than the circular and rotating moves of the "soft styles" such as Kung Fu.

Until it traveled to Japan from Okinawa in 1921, karate, meaning "empty hand," was called *te*, or hand, and was an art practiced by the peasants who were defending themselves from the oppression of the warrior class or from brigands. The board breaking was practiced because these oppressors often wore interlocking wooden armor, not metal as in Europe. The idea was to be able to damage or even break through that armor with bare hands and feet.

In Japan, the Samurai or warrior caste embraced karate. Though primarily a weaponless self-defense system, some styles incorporated a few weapons. Until it reached Japan, most of the weapons used were actually farm implements or tools. The Japanese added swords and archery to the mix.

Bryan's first exposure thrilled him. One of the black belts, a *sempai*, or a senior student, called the class to order, and they lined up in rows according to the colors of their belts. The sensei or instructor entered the room from a door in the rear, and the sempai shouted, "Bow!" And all the students complied. The sensei then directed the sempai to lead the class in warm-ups, which consisted of stretching and loosening each body area. Then they assumed a "horse stance" with one clenched fist extended forward at arms length, palm side down, and the other fist couched against the waist, palm side up. Following the sempai's lead, punches were thrown with each hand alternately, accompanied by a shout, or *kiai*, at each thrust. Next, assorted blocks were done, accompanied by the kiai, and finally, a variety of kicks were accomplished. This all took about twenty minutes or so.

The sempai then led kata, a series of pre-coreographed moves. The basic kata consisted of punches, kicks, and blocks performed in unison moving an I pattern. The sensei monitored this activity, correcting and improving the techniques of the students.

At this point, the sensei took over and began to practice a more advanced kata with the more senior students and the beginners observing from the sidelines. He then directed these senior students to form groups of the beginners and teach them the advanced kata. In this manner, everyone learned more by teaching.

The class was then paired up by ranking, and they practiced alternately attacking and defending using predetermined punches, kicks, and blocks. The moves were made at half speed, and making no hard contact on your opponent was stressed. The sensei and sempai circulated between the pairs, commenting and correcting the moves.

Bryan noted that most of the girls in the class were at least as adept as the boys and several of them were even more skilled than boys of similar rank, particularly in high kicking and spinning moves. There was neither differentiation nor discrimination when the students were paired either, and the girls more than held their own.

Bryan was convinced after auditing one class and signed up for lessons. Classes were scheduled every weeknight, an early class for beginners often taught by senior students and a later class for intermediate and advanced students taught by the sensei and assisted by a sempai. Usually, one night per week was set aside for sparring at full speed, and some safety equipment was used, padded hand and foot gear, to minimize injuries. At least once a month, many of the students traveled as a group to local martial arts tournaments to compete and spectate.

The young man threw himself into the training, attending as many classes each week as his schedule permitted. He was involved in school activities, mostly athletics, but there were few conflicts. He progressed rapidly, his natural athletic ability enabling him to conquer advanced techniques at a faster rate than most. Contrary to his mother's concerns about his grades suffering, they actually improved markedly.

His fascination with karate never waned, and by the time he was sixteen, Bryan had achieved the rank of black belt, first degree. He was tall and a little bigger than most boys his age and competed in tournaments against adult men. As his skills had increased, he began to win, place, or show in both *kumite* (fighting) and kata (forms). During his senior year in high school, Bryan was tested for and was awarded his second degree black belt.

Upon graduation from high school in the upper ten percent of his class in grade-point average, Bryan was awarded an Army ROTC scholarship to his parents' alma mater. He had selected this means of paying for his education as an assertion of his independence so his parents could afford to provide his younger brother with a quality education at a major university. Jason had shown a great talent and desire for the sciences and hoped for a career in biological research, which would require an advanced degree from a hallmark school.

A small cadre of fellow ROTC students developed a mutual interest in survival skills. They spent many weekends rafting, canoeing, and camping in the wilderness. Bryan was drawn to these outings and fit in well with his companions, often finding himself the leader of their activities. He continued his karate training with a martial arts club at the school where he was exposed to a number of different styles of karate, kung fu, tae kwon do, and tang soo do.

During summer breaks in college, Bryan chose to attend various army training schools as an ROTC officer candidate, one of which was airborne training at Fort Benning, Georgia, and preliminary ranger training at Fort Bragg, North Carolina. Upon graduation and with his commission as a second lieutenant in the US Army, Bryan was sent to a basic platoon leaders course, then to ranger training at Fort Bragg. As in the past, Brian enjoyed the challenges offered by the intense physical regimen, in which he excelled.

THE CHIEF

He Who Faces West bore the weight of his forty summers lightly. His robust physique and energy were that of a man many years his junior. He could still wrestle with the strongest of his tribe and hold his own in a distance race though he was a step slower in the sprints. He was tall for his people, with broad shoulders, deep chest, and the long, slim legs of a runner. His long, slender arms were well muscled. His face bore well the seams and creases of his forty years, as well as the marks of his clan totem on his cheeks. He wore his hair in twin braids down his back, having eschewed the vanity-influenced styles of the younger warriors for ease of maintenance.

Faces West was the tribal chief, the political leader of his people, chosen by the elders after it was apparent that the people listened to his counsel and respected his wisdom. In his younger days, he had been a warrior, a war leader, and later, a war chief. He had counted coup many times and had shown bravery in the face of the enemy, but more importantly, he was a smart man, a good judge of people, and a husband and father of kindness and understanding.

His clan-group of The People called Red Talkers, or Cheyenne, by their northern plains rivals, The Dakota, had just settled into their summer encampment in the heart of their hunting grounds. Scouts had been sent out to locate the buffalo on which their survival depended, while other hunters had been dispatched to locate immediate sustenance. The women were organizing the camp. Lodges had been set up in the proscribed manner, the principal chief's dwelling in the center of the village, the others, by status, radiating out from there. The exception was the lodge of the shaman, which was at the eastern edge of the camp. All the lodge entrances faced the rising sun.

This morning, a group of hunters had returned with three antelopes for the communal pot, so there would be fresh meat in the camp tonight, a pleasant relief from the winter and traveling diet of pemmican and early season tubers.

Faces West was relaxing against his backrest in front of his lodge, contemplating a tasty antelope stew, which his wife, Many Robes, would prepare soon when he was approached by He Who Has Made Many Coups, a warrior and war leader. Many Coups was a loud and impetuous man, given to quick anger, but he had proved himself in battle, and the younger warriors were prone to follow him on forays against their enemies. He was shorter in stature than the average but quite strong and burly, and his hair was worn in an upright roach, proclaiming his warrior status.

Many Coups said he wanted to lead a small group of young warriors on a raid against the Omaha, many days travel to the northeast. They expected to take some women prisoners but not engage the Omaha warriors unless their stealthy mission was discovered.

Faces West realized that the young warriors were restless after the long winter and trek to the summer encampment, but he also realized that there were war parties from their enemies who would be similarly restless. With several hunting parties out, less than a quarter of the men were in camp, and even a small group such as proposed by Many Coups would leave the camp nearly undefended and vulnerable to the early spring raiding parties. He declined Many Coups's request to raid. The war leader stalked off angrily. Faces West had faced this anger frequently. Sometimes, it was hard to be patient with the warrior, but he was because Many Coups's value to their tribe outweighed problems caused by the man's childish tantrums. He leaned against the backrest to contemplate other problems of leadership.

In the far distant past, a strong, populous, war-like people had pushed The People from their ancestral lands near the Great Water. The people were pushed because their leaders had chosen to move rather than fight a battle they probably wouldn't win against greater numbers. The People were farmers then; though they were strong, their warrior skills had eroded over generations of peaceful agronomy.

In moving, The People "lost the corn," their farming ways, exchanging them for the nomadic life of the Great Plains, avoiding conflicts by moving, ever moving westward, following the game herds on which their lives now depended. The life of a hunter-gatherer could not support a concentrated population, so they broke up into family-clans, seldom numbering more than fifteen or twenty families. They came together one time a year in a great encampment to renew ties, cement relationships, and allow the young men the chance to meet marriageable women from other clans

The Great Plains were not without hazards though, and from the west and south came hostile raiding parties, seeking food, weapons, and women. It would be weeks before the great summer encampment would occur, and Faces West had more concerns that the restlessness of the younger men.

FINDING THE PEOPLE

Maybe I can backtrack the hunters who ambushed that antelope, thought Bryan. He returned to the site of his kill and cast about for sign. The tracks of the herd seemed to have come from the northwest, in the general direction of the headwaters of the creek by his calculation. He followed a short distance to make sure, then returned to his temporary camp to gather his meager positions, which now included the dried meat that he wrapped in the somewhat softened hide. He also took the stomach of the beast that he had cleaned.

He spent the remainder of the day following the meandering trail of the small herd of antelope. As the sun began to dip over the horizon, he sought shelter where he could build a fire and camp for the night. He was still only a short distance from the creek, and he headed that way. At the creekside, he knelt and washed out the ram's stomach on which he had left a piece of both the entrance and exit intestine. Around one of these protrusions, he tied a small strip of hide, effectively sealing that exit. He submersed the bladder in the clear running stream, nearly filling it with water. He then tied a rawhide strip around the neck of his water bottle. With more rawhide strips, he fashioned a carrying strap. After drinking his fill, he shouldered the bag and moved to the campsite he had selected.

A short time later, the oncoming darkness found Bryan seated before a small fire in a hollow amongst the trees. He had rehydrated several strips of antelope jerky in a bark bowl filled water and was now grilling them on sticks over the fire. The smell of the cooking meat was intoxicating.

Throughout the day, Bryan had frequent feelings of being watched. Several times he had looked around, once even going to the top or a knoll and scanning the horizon for signs of movement or other evidence of a presence, but he spotted nothing. As his meat heated through, he again had the feeling. In the gloom beyond the fire, he saw a movement, but as he stared at the spot where he though it came from, he saw nothing. He continued to peer at the shadows until the hiss of meat juices hitting the fire brought him back to his cooking. His meal finished, he bedded down in a nest of leaves.

His sleep was interrupted by a recurring dream of an old man sitting before a small fire and mumbling incantations in a strange tongue. The flickering firelight showed a seamed face surrounded by lank gray-white hair. The face was broad with high cheekbones and deep-set dark eyes. The firelight did not show the surroundings where the old man was sitting, but Bryan got the impression that he was in some type of enclosure. There was something hypnotic about the chanting, some sort of message that the old man was trying to get through.

He rolled out of his bed the next morning just before dawn. The air was chilly, but he wasn't uncomfortable. Bryan did his daily dozen stretching exercises, loosening and warming his muscles. The sun was still below the horizon, but it was light enough to see the animals' trail clearly. After a long drink from the stream, he gathered his meager possessions and set out on the antelopes' back trail.

The tracks were easy to follow in the soft loam. The trail moved away from the stream, out onto the prairie. Bryan kept himself oriented by frequently checking his surroundings. The location of the stream was visible by the trees lining the banks. He estimated that he was traveling northwest by the position of the sunrise. About midday, he found where the hunters had ambushed the antelope. Their tracks were deeper in the turf, indicating they were running hard, and backtracking, and he found where several animals had been brought down. Blood and viscera on the matted grasses showed where the hunters had butchered at least three pronghorns. There were footprints around the site, but Bryan couldn't tell how many people had been there, but it appeared as if there were at least three or four.

The tracks of the hunters were easy to follow as they were burdened by the added weight of their prey and left deep footprints in the soft soil. Topping a small rise, he could see the trail from way the grass was bent by their passage. This track led straight across the grasslands toward a tree line several miles distant. Bryan quickened his pace to a dogtrot. The trail was following low-lying ground, never along any of the low ridges that abounded on the seemingly flat terrain. It was obvious that the hunters were moving fairly fast despite their burdens but were careful not to expose themselves.

Bryan didn't like to leave the stream behind, but he had water in his bladder canteen, so he wouldn't thirst. He arrived at the tree line and found where the hunters had built a fire, cooked something, and bedded down. Bryan figured he was about a day's travel behind the hunters. There was a small brook running amongst the trees, so he topped of his canteen and headed on at a quicker pace. He had a couple hours more of daylight and thought he would be able to make up some distance on the hunting party before camping for the night. He chewed on a piece of jerky as he ran. His feet were callused from his karate training, and he barely felt any discomfort from any dirt clods or pebbles his feet fell on as he sped along.

During the night, comfortable in his "nest" in the roots of a tree, he heard wolves howling in the distance. He figured that a pack was gathering for a hunt or maybe just howling for the pleasure of it. He seemed to recollect that wolves avoided men, but he slept rather lightly that night, awakening frequently to listen, then dozed off again.

He was up before daybreak, breakfasted on dried meat and a long drink of water. He then set out on the trail of the hunters.

It was midafternoon when Bryan topped a low rise and glimpsed the village in the shallow valley about three hundred yards below. There were twenty or so teepees, of the type he had seen in old photographs of the American West, laid out in an orderly fashion along the banks of a small stream. The afternoon had been warm, and the sides of the lodges were rolled up exposing the lodgepole framework. Wisps of smoke rose through the open flaps at the peaks from what was probably cooking fires. Bryan hunkered down in the grass and watched the activity in the village.

There were figures moving around the cooking fires in most of the lodges and he assumed these were women by their dress. Children of various ages were playing along the stream, their shouts and laughter coming faintly to his ears. They seemed to be playing some sort of game-of-tag and were having a great time. Three antelope carcasses were hung from poles near the center of the village and were being butchered by several women. By the look of the remains, much of the meat had already been cut away and probably distributed...explaining the cooking activity in the lodges.

A small group of men were seated under a large cottonwood tree and appeared to be discussing something. The central figure, a large, imposing man, was seated at the bole of the tree and was gesturing as he spoke. The others seemed to wait respectfully until the man stopped speaking. Then another man took up the discussion while the others listened. Bryan couldn't hear the sounds but could tell whom the speaker was by the attention paid by the others, that and the gestures that seemed to accompany the words.

He lay there for a while and contemplated his options. He was unsure how the people below would react to the sudden appearance of a naked man. He had to make an unthreatening approach yet be confident in his attitude but display no aggressive moves. He slid back from the crest and gathered his goods, hung his canteen bladder from his shoulder so that the bladder concealed some of his frontal nakedness, thrust his throwing stick and knife into the rawhide belt, grasped his staff, walked slowly over the ridge, and began the descent toward the village.

He was noticed immediately, and a low murmur came to his ears as the group of men arose and moved toward him to the edge of the village. Some younger warriors had quickly armed themselves with spears and hurried to the front of the group assuming a defensive stance. The playing children stopped and then hurried behind the line of men while the women paused in their work and watched him come down the slope.

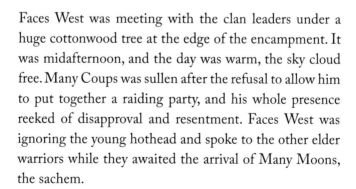

Faces West was meeting with the clan leaders under a huge cottonwood tree at the edge of the encampment. It was midafternoon, and the day was warm, the sky cloud free. Many Coups was sullen after the refusal to allow him to put together a raiding party, and his whole presence reeked of disapproval and resentment. Faces West was ignoring the young hothead and spoke to the other elder warriors while they awaited the arrival of Many Moons, the sachem.

A hubbub arose at the far side of the village. Faces West and the others arose as one and hurried toward the sounds of excited talking. A group of women and children were clustered together, jabbering and looking toward the hillside beyond the village. A very tall naked man was striding purposefully down the slope toward the group. The stranger was carrying a staff in one hand and had the other held up in the sign of peace. Around his waist was a belt through which was thrust a throwing stick and knife while a water bladder was hanging from one shoulder and a hide bundle from the other. There was an air of confidence about his person despite his lack of clothing or weaponry.

The group of warriors moved through the group of women and children and spread out a bit as they awaited the arrival of the stranger. It was a practice of The People to accept friendly, though with some reservations, any strangers who approached them openly. The group of warriors were not armed and had only personal knives that they were never without, except for Many Coups, who, it seemed, was always carrying some weapon. Today it was a long hunting spear. Because there were no threatening moves by the stranger and because of the number of warriors around him, Faces West wasn't alarmed.

When the stranger was about thirty paces away, Faces West moved out from the group of men to greet the man, but Many Coups edged past him with his spear at the ready. Before Faces West could order him back, the hotheaded warrior had attacked the stranger, thrusting hard at him with his spear. What happened then was a surprise to all.

Instead of dodging the spear, the stranger parried the thrust with his forearm and then grasped the spear shaft as it passed his side, pulling it strongly. At the same time, his other hand closed and snapped forward, catching the off-balanced Many Coups a mighty blow in the face with the fist. The hothead fell to the ground, stunned.

The stranger lay down the spear and the staff and then held up both hands to show they were empty. Faces West motioned for two warriors to attend to Many Coups, who was just beginning to stand groggily. He then signed for the stranger to follow him and turned toward his lodge.

In his mind, Faces West was almost sure that the tall stranger was the Spirit Warrior foretold by Many Moons, the sachem. The big man was much lighter skinned than The People though he did have the same dark hair. His eyes, however, were piercing blue, a shade never seen amongst The People or any of the other tribes they had encountered since their beginnings. The ease with which he handled Many Coups attack showed the prowess of a warrior. At his lodge, he entered and bade the stranger be seated on his right as he lowered himself to his soft seat beside the fire pit in the center of the circular lodge.

A crowd of people had gathered outside the chief's lodge, easily visible with the rolled up sides of the teepee. The chief spoke to one of the young men, telling him to ask the shaman to come to the lodge. He then called for his senior wife to bring something for them to eat.

THE OLD SHAMAN MEETS THE PALE MAN

He Who Has Lived Many Moons was older than anyone else in the clan; in fact, he was probably older than anyone living amongst all the clans of The People. He was so old that he remembered firsthand stories of the migration from the northern lakes region to the central plains. They had left their ancestral home because of conflict with the Dakotas, who had later followed them, themselves pushed by the Chippewa, but had settled farther to the north. Many Moons was a shaman, a practitioner of magic, a caster of spells, a seer with the gift of sight, and a medicine dreamer. He was the religious leader of his people.

As a youth, he had followed the ways of the other youth, learning the art of war, because in their small numbers, everyone had to be a warrior. He had hunted and gone through the rites of passage from boy to man like all of the others; the vision quest, the dances, and folkways of his people, he had learned. But Many Moons had been different, always. From an early age, he had been visited by many dreams that often foretold of events critical to his people. His visions and spirituality had caused The People to give him his manhood name of He Who Sees Far. In the manner of his people, when his life had changed direction, he had sought a vision and a new name. Now, due in part to his age, but mainly from a vision which had visited him more than twenty summers ago, he was Many Moons.

The People had many myths and legends about their past and about their future. A recurring figure in many of these tales was that of the Pale Man, one who could be summoned when the tribe was beset by enemies, famine, or in need of guidance. During the great migration of The People, the Pale Man had come in a dream to Sees Far, as he was known then, and counseled him the take The People to the southwest. Only the members of his clan-group would follow this advice as they had seen up close the accuracy of the young mystic's premonitions. Other clan-groups had elected to move due west and had hardly settled when the Dakota had pushed into their hunting grounds and drove them out. For many years now, the northern clan-groups of The People had been beset by frequent skirmishes with the Dakota, holding their own, but suffering from the constant pressure.

The Pale Man had appeared to Many Moons since that time, often bearing a spear in one hand and the wampum belt of peace in the other. Many Moons often had good counsel from the Pale Man, and now his clan-group almost felt that this dream person was their own special totem. He had guided them in the changes in their lifestyle necessitated by their move to the plains. They "lost the corn," as their elders had put it, and took up hunting full time for their sustenance. Their villages had to be mobile now, so they were shown how to design and build their lodges from poles and buffalo hides and also how to hunt the great beasts that became the basis of their economy.

Now, once again, Many Moons need the counsel of the Pale Man. The fierce Omaha people were pushing from the east, into the hunting grounds of The People. Hunters from their village had been picking up signs of these people and on several occasions there had been minor skirmishes between hunting parties, but as yet, there had been no war parties sent out by either group, but it was only a matter to time before the raiding began. Of the clan elders, only Many Moons was part of the great migration from the lake country, but all had heard the tales of the ongoing war with the Dakota people, and most of them wanted to move once again. Many of the younger men wanted to stay and fight or even initiate the conflict by raids on the Omaha. The camp was becoming split, and all were looking to Many Moons for a sign.

For weeks now, Many Moons had been praying to the Great Spirit, purifying himself in the sweat lodge, fasting for a vision, focusing his entire being, and all that he had learned over the decades on bringing help from the Pale Man. He knew the time for a sign was imminent. Last night, the Pale Man had appeared to the shaman, again bearing the spear and the peace belt. He did not speak, but using hand signs, the spear and belt hovering in the air beside him, he told of the coming war with the Omaha people. Even if The People migrated again, the trouble would go with them because there were the Pawnees to the west and Kiowa to the south. It was time to make a stand and win their right to live unmolested. They must prepare themselves for the conflict by storing more food, making new weapons, training the inexperienced young men and boys.

The Pale Man continued to sign. He would come to them to help them in their time of need, and when it passed, he would leave them. Many Moons was relieved, but he kept this knowledge to himself, awaiting the coming of the Pale Man.

The old man heard faintly the hubbub in the camp, and after a time, there was a polite scratching at his teepee entrance.

"Come in," he responded, and the flap was pulled back and a young warrior entered respectfully.

With strongly contained excitement, the young brave told him that the chief has asked for the shaman's presence in his teepee. There was a stranger in the camp, a pale man, and he was at the chief's lodge. The shaman was thrilled. A pale man had appeared, and so soon after his dream. He rose and followed the young brave.

When Many Moons entered the chief's teepee and saw Bryan, he was stunned, even though he had been expecting his arrival. Here indeed was the Pale Man of his dreams.

His eyes took in the pale skin, heavily muscled frame, and dark hair, and when the man looked up at him, the pale blue eyes. He had never seen such eyes before, not even in the dreams, for the Pale Man's face had always been shadowed, his eyes not visible.

The chief, Faces West, spoke to him with courtesy, offering him the seat of honor on the chief's right. He seated himself on the robe the chief's wife placed there for him and waited while Faces West got out his pipe and filled it with an aromatic mixture of tobacco and herbs. His senior wife lighted it with a coal from the fire held between two sticks.

The chief drew deeply on the pipe and then blew smoke to the four winds—east, north, west, and south. Then he blew smoke at the sky and again at the earth, completing the honoring of all six sacred directions. The pipe was passed to the shaman, who repeated the honors, and then the pipe was passed to Bryan, who had watched closely the ritual followed by the two Indians.

The old shaman was very relieved to see the Pale Man show his peaceful intentions by following the ritual. He then spoke to his chief.

"I have seen the coming of this Pale Man for many moons, and most recently, last night, he came to me and said that he would help us with our coming war with the Omaha."

The chief responded, "He is a warrior of great skill. You should have seen how easily he vanquished Many Coups, handling him as if he were an inexperienced boy." He continued, "But he does not speak our tongue."

"We must teach him, then," said the shaman. "We must assign someone to show him the hand signs and to speak our language."

"White Bull is the best choice," replied the chief. "He has shown an aptitude for languages, learning Pawnee and Kiowa from two captive slaves. I'll summon him." Motioning to the young brave who had remained standing at the door, he dispatched him to bring White Bull to the chief's teepee.

Bryan had been following the conversation of the two men, not understanding a word but knowing that he was the topic. When the old shaman had entered, Bryan had been startled. Here was the old man who had appeared in his dreams, and he was sure of it. The same strong wrinkled face, long straight hair shot with gray, and the dark, probing eyes. The old man even acted like he had seen Bryan too, his eyes widening at the first sight of the white man seated by the chief. He dearly wished he could communicate with the shaman. Maybe then, he would then find out where he was and how and why he was here, but most importantly, how he could get home again!

While they waited for the arrival of White Bull, the wife of Faces West bustled around the fire, dishing up stew for the men to eat, deferentially serving the old shaman first, then Bryan and her husband.

The stew was savory, with chunks of meat in it and bits of herbs and wild onions floating in the thick broth. Bryan was so hungry he could scarcely contain himself waiting for the chief to be served before he dug in with the bone spoon provided with the bowl, which appeared to be made from dried buffalo hide. The aroma of the stew made his mouth water, and his stomach growled, much to his embarrassment. It was delicious. The chief watched with pleasure as Bryan made short work of the stew. He motioned for his wife to fill the Pale Man's bowl again. Before Bryan had finished the second helping of stew, there was a scratch at the door flap, and a young man entered at the chief's acknowledgement.

White Bull was tall, nearly as tall as Bryan, and well built. His hair fell into two braids over the front of his shoulders. Unlike many of the other young men Bryan had seen, he did not affect a pompadour or other flamboyant hair style but had his simply parted in the middle. The ends of his braids were wrapped in some kind of fur and hung over the front of his shoulders. A single feather hung from the back. His smooth skin was light brown and marked only by the tattoo of his totem on his left breast. His alert dark eyes took in the pale stranger and then returned to his clan leader, awaiting the reason for his summons.

Faces West bade him be seated, and his wife filled another bowl with the stew that she handed to the young warrior. The others continued eating, the silence broken only by an occasional polite belch from the Indians. When they were done and the eating vessels put aside, Faces West looked at White Bull.

"You have learned well the tongues of the Pawnee and Kiowa. You have acquitted yourself well on the war trail and as a hunter. I have a challenge for you which I have faith that you will handle as well as you have everything else." The chief paused dramatically. "I want you to teach the language of The People to the Pale Man here." He indicated Bryan with a nod of his head. "Our Shaman has been told of his coming, that he will help us in our confrontation with the Omaha, but we need to be able to talk with him to learn his lessons." The chief went on, "Teach him to sign with his hands. It will make your task easier."

The chief further said, "Your lodge is not crowded. Make room for him there, and provide him with food, clothing, and teaching."

The young man grunted an assent. The chief made Bryan to understand through hand signs that he was to accompany the young warrior.

White Bull's lodge was home to his mother, his sister, and him. A buffalo had gored his father during a hunt several years before, and after lingering for four days, he had joined the Great Spirit. He had been a good hunter and warrior and had taught his son well. White Bull had become the man of his lodge at the tender age of seventeen, and he had become a good provider.

He had always been mature for his age and had assumed his responsibilities well. His mother and older sister had deferred to his judgment in most matters, but they totally ran the lodge. His father's high ranking meant that their lodge was situated close to the inner circle, near the lodge of their chief. White Bull had earned the respect of the village elders, thus their lodge was still in this place, even after his father's death.

A handsome man, White Bull received many an admiring glance from eligible maidens, but none of them had caught his eye. He was not immune to feminine charms, but other matters occupied his mind. He had been visited on occasion by a dream in which the Great White Bull, from whom he had taken his adult name, came to him and advised him that he was to become a great leader of his people, but before that time, he was to go on a long and arduous journey. There had been no further explanation, only the repeated message of the long journey toward the setting sun.

White Bull's life was typical of a young warrior. He hunted almost daily, mostly for small and medium game, but on occasion, all of the men hunted buffalo together. When he wasn't hunting, he was repairing or making weapons. Most of the points on his arrows and spears were of finely knapped flint, but his most prized possession was his war ax with a head of copper, obtained by trading with a tribe of metal workers who lived on the western edge of the Great Lakes to the northeast. These people had discovered deposits of nearly pure copper, which, over a long period of time, they learned to hammer into assorted tools and weapons that they traded for furs, meat, corn, and other necessities. Even the flint for spear and arrows had been traded for since there were few flint deposits in the hunting area of The People. A flourishing trade existed among the tribes of the plains and the knappers of the flint.

Now, with Bryan in tow, White Bull headed toward his teepee. When they arrived, he opened the flap and motioned for the pale one to follow him. Inside, his mother and sister were sewing on skin garments, it being too early to prepare the evening meal. They did not show a startled reaction to Bryan's presence, having already heard the hubbub about the Pale Man and how he vanquished Many Coups, but they looked him over covertly while their son and brother explained to them the task laid out by the chief.

White Bull spoke to his mother who went to the rolled up buffalo robes around the outer wall of the tent and got some skin garments that she brought back to her son. White Bull indicated to Bryan to put on the breechcloth and leggings. Bryan hesitated momentarily, then put aside his modesty. He removed the remnants of the poorly tanned, hardened, antelope hide and grass rope, then donned the breechcloth and leggings, which fit him moderately well, other than being a little short in the legs.

The Indians couldn't help but notice how pale his skin was under the antelope skin, but they feigned disinterest. Indians too darkened where their bodies were exposed to the sun, but none of their unexposed flesh was as pale as that they had just glimpsed. This was a pale man indeed!

With Bryan dressed, White Bull indicated to him to be seated and then began the rudimentary training in the Tongue of The People, first by picking up an item, a tool or weapon, or other implement and giving the name, also showing the sign for the item in the hand language common to most American Indians. Bryan caught on quickly as to what was expected and soon was trying to repeat the words after his tutor. His verbal fumblings caused great mirth amongst his hosts, who, at first, stifled their grins but finally broke out into laughter. By dinnertime, Bryan had a vocabulary of a dozen or so names of weapons, tools, and utensils.

During the lessons, the women had prepared dinner, another meaty, aromatic stew of antelope, wild herbs, and tubers. They ate, the women talking animatedly all the while. Later, White Bull showed his guest which pallet was his, and they turned in for the night.

Though exhausted from the ordeal of the day, Bryan lay awake for some time before he was able to sleep. He kept going over the events of the past few days and the circumstances of his being in this time and place, and he still couldn't make any sense of it at all. He was worried about his family and friends but was secretly a little proud of having survived the first real tests of his skills. These Indians, Bryan was sure they were Cheyenne, were a clean, handsome people, who fit in with their environment. Their acceptance of him, at least by most of them, surprised Bryan, but he knew that he could expect problems from Roach Lock down the road. His weariness finally overcame his inquiring mind and he slept.

THE TRAINING OF BRYAN

Bryan awoke to stirring in the teepee. The younger of the two women was rolling up her buffalo robe pallet. He saw that she was naked, but the light was so dim that all he could make out was that she was slender and clean limbed. Her small, pointed breasts swayed slightly as she gathered her clothes, the dark areola barely visible in the darkness. His own modesty made him want to close his eyes, but he didn't. The young woman stirred up the fire and added some fuel. As it flared up, Bryan turned his head toward the wall until he heard more movements indicating that she was dressing. He turned back as she was straightening her deerskin dress and found her looking straight into his eyes. Her gaze was very direct, whereas the few other women he had observed kept their eyes downcast in the presence of the men. This one was almost challenging in her look, and her bearing was most regal. It was all over too quickly, and the young woman went out, leaving the entrance flap pulled back so the morning sun would light the lodge's interior.

He did not know the relationship between his new tutor and the women of the household, but he assumed that the older one was his mother and the younger his wife. He had avoided a close examination of them the night before, not wanting to offend them or appear rude as he didn't know the ways of these Indians.

The young woman returned, rummaged in a corner, then moved to the entry flap, and left the teepee with a leather pail in each hand. Bryan had the impression of tall, slender attractiveness. She had fine features and a full-lipped mouth with straight, white teeth. Her raven hair was worn in braids that hung down her back. Her voice, on the few occasions she had spoken last night, was low and throaty.

There was more stirring, and soon, both the other occupants of the tent were rising, dressing, and rolling their pallets. Bryan hastily donned the clothes he had been given the previous evening and followed the brave outside to some bushes near the creek where they both relived themselves. The young woman returned about the same time they did, carrying two pails of water, most of which was dumped into a leather cauldron which was suspended from a rack near the now blazing fire. Using two sticks, several large stones were eased from the fireplace and dropped into the water, sending steam into the air. Each of the others took a bowl of the heated water outside and washed themselves. Bryan followed suit and found the hand bath very refreshing. Thin strips of meat, probably antelope, had been skewered and placed near the fire. When they were done with the light breakfast, the young brave signed for Bryan to follow and left the teepee.

As he followed White Bull down to the stream by the camp, Bryan reviewed what he had seen of the weapons and the other aspects of the encampment. The flint-tipped arrows and spears, abundance of large dogs, but lack of horses led him to believe that somehow he had landed in a place and time before the arrival of Europeans in the New World. How he had gotten here was a mystery, but he had better adapt and make the best of the situation until he awoke or was snatched back to his own world and time.

When they got to the stream bank, the brave seated himself and motioned for Bryan to do the same, and then the lessons began again. First, a repeat of the words learned yesterday. The young host was showing pleasure that Bryan needed little prompting. Then they began a series of new nouns. During the rest of the morning, they moved about the camp, pausing when the Indian would point to some object and utter the name, repeating it slowly, syllable by syllable, until Bryan was able to repeat a reasonably pronounced facsimile. In this manner, his knowledge of the Tongue progressed rapidly.

At some point during the next few days, they progressed to action words, verbs. During the evenings, White Bull began to teach Bryan the universal sign language of the American Indian. Bryan caught on very quickly, and in short order, they were able to carry on rudimentary conversations, reverting to sign language when words failed the white man.

In time, Bryan learned that he was amongst a clan of The People, as they referred to themselves, headed by He Who Faces West, the chief or political leader of the clan. The religious figure was the old shaman, He Who Has Lived Many Moons. He also learned that the war leader he had bested was Many Coups, a proud and arrogant man who would probably seek some sort of retribution.

Every day when he first awoke, Bryan would stretch out, then practice kata or forms for half an hour or so. White Bull would watch with interest, and soon, he was trying to emulate the tall, pale man he now called Bry-Yan. Bryan could see his interest and started to teach him the basic moves of karate, beginning with blocks—*gedan barai uke*, the down-block; *agee uke*, the rising block; *shuto uke*, the knife-hand block; and inside and outside blocks. Then he moved to teaching the hand strikes—*oi zuke*, front punch; *kara zuke*, reverse punch; *shuto zuke*, knife-hand strike; *ippon nukite*, spear-hand thrust; and *empi and uraken zuke*, the elbow and backfist strikes. Finally, he began to teach the basic foot techniques—front, side, roundhouse, reverse, and turning kicks.

When White Bull began to master the basic techniques of the blocks, punches, and kicks, Bryan began to teach him the forms or kata. These progressed from basic patterns involving one or two blocks, kicks, and strikes up to very involved forms, often of fifty or more moves and a dozen techniques. In most systems of karate, there are as many as thirty forms, each being progressively more complex. The forms are grouped loosely by belt rank—low-colored belts, high-colored belts, brown belt, and finally the most complex, black-belt kata. The forms were the old masters' means of practicing their art and many of the moves were often only clues to what the real moves were... The masters jealously guarded the techniques they secretly developed.

In the weeks that followed, White Bull taught Bryan his Tongue, and Bryan taught White Bull his martial art, all of which did not go unnoticed by the others of the tribe. When Bryan advanced White Bull to sparring, kumite, and defending against weapons, the Indian began to see the reasons for the various moves and took great pleasure in being able to defend himself against Bryan's half-speed attacks.

One evening, after their meal, White Bull and Bryan were leaning against their backrests when the Indian spoke.

"I have been approached by several of the young warriors." He paused for a moment for Bryan to digest this information. "They have watched with interest our training in your hand and foot fighting." Again a pause. "If it is not too much to expect, they would like to join us in our training."

Bryan framed his reply carefully in his hesitant grasp of the Tongue. "I will be happy to have them join us." He looked at White Bull to see if he phrased it correctly.

White Bull beamed with pleasure. "It will please them."

The next morning, there were six others to stretch out with White Bull and Bryan. The following morning, there were ten, and each day thereafter, a few more showed up until there were twenty-five students, including several that were little more than boys. They trained with Bryan each morning for about an hour and a half. After class, they would disperse to their various duties and activities, but Bryan often saw the younger ones practicing techniques and forms while they played amongst the village teepees.

In teaching his karate, Bryan found his vocabulary in the Tongue increasing daily by translating from Japanese and English each of the moves of the martial art.

MANY COUPS

Many Coups had received his adult name, He Who Counts Many Coups, from a quest during his nineteenth year. He had been shown a vision of himself as a great war leader of his people, counting coups many times on his foes, his war bonnet of coup feathers hanging almost to the ground.

He was a strongly made, athletic young man who had always excelled at every physical activity he engaged in. He had a good eye for throwing a spear, shooting an arrow. He was fleet of foot and a good wrestler, able to hold his own against most of the other boys and even many of the men while he was still an untested fifteen-year-old.

He had strong, handsome features and wore his long, glistening black locks in a high pompadour in front and a single long, loosely braided strand in the back. He is of medium height, and his confident carriage made him seem taller. His confidence was often tinged with the arrogance that comes from easy successes.

When he had been moved to attack the pale stranger, despite the counseling against it by Faces West, he had been sure of an easy victory and another scalp to decorate his coupstick. He was very surprised to find himself bested, and so easily, by an unarmed man. His shame was complete when his still groggy form was carried back to his lodge and unceremoniously dumped on a pallet.

He brooded on the matter for several days until his mind, unable to accept the easy defeat, convinced him that he was the victim of magic. His confidence was restored though slightly bruised and more humble, so he began to move among the people again.

He was dismayed to learn that the chief and old shaman had allowed the pale man to stay among The People. In fact, he was living in the lodge of White Bull and his sister, Strong Woman, on whom Many Coups had designs.

He began to watch the morning activities of Bryan and White Bull and finally the entire group of karate trainees. It disturbed him very much.

He was of the Running Dog Lodge of The People, a group more inclined to the war trail than any other activity. He and the other members of this warrior society were often raiding on other tribes, particularly on the Pawnee, their traditional enemies, and on the Dakota to the north. Most of their raids were to count coups, not to kill their opponents, and to take valuables, often girls or women to be used as slaves and sometimes for wives.

Now, Many Coups had a problem to place before his society—how to deal with the pale man because Many Coups saw him as a threat, possibly a rival, and there was his humiliation to avenge. Most of the Running Dog

Lodge members were impressed by their most aggressive member and followed his lead, but there were a few of the warriors who had more level heads, so there was much discussion over the way to react to this pale man.

Most of the lodge members had seen how easily Many Coups had been bested, and no one was particularly anxious to challenge the pale man directly, but no one was quite sure how to defeat him. The few who had calmer heads counseled against any action; in fact, they felt that maybe they could learn something from this stranger as was evidenced by the growing training group he was leading.

Many Coups was enraged by what he perceived as disloyalty to him by these few, but he had the good sense not to alienate them. Instead, he decided to bide his time and await the opening to destroy or discredit this pale stranger. In order to avoid a confrontation, he planned a raid on the Pawnee. A hunting party had brought back information of the signs of a small village about three days travel to the northwest. This was closer than the Pawnee usually got into the hunting grounds of The People, so Many Coups figured that he should teach them a lesson.

With five of his lodge brothers, it was decided to leave in the morning before the dawn. He normally would have conferred with Faces West and gone to the shaman for a good luck spell, but with the chief expressing his disapproval earlier, he decided to go without permission or his blessing.

In the early morning, the group of six met at the lodge of Many Coups. They were carrying short war spears, bow cases and quivers of arrows, war clubs with stone heads, and their ever-present knives. Each had a medicine bag on a thong around their necks and a small pouch of pemmican. Other than that, they will live off the land. They wore breechcloths, leggings, and shirts, all of buckskin, and leather belts into which are thrust the knife cases and war clubs. Bow cases and quivers were slung across their backs, leaving their hands free except for their spears.

They departed from the village at a dogtrot. The only sound was the slap-slapping of their feet on the packed ground, but even that disappeared when they got to the sound muffling grass. They could run this way all day, pausing only to drink or if a hunting opportunity presented itself, stopping then only if it was something they could carry with them until they stopped for the evening.

THE VISION OF MANY MOONS

Many Moons could hardly remember when he had the first vision-dream of the Pale Man; it had been so long ago. At first, he had appeared in a nighttime dream in which Many Moons was hunting. He dreamt that he had been gone for many days without seeing any game. He had searched on the plains for buffalo and antelope, in the creek bottoms for deer and rabbits, and in the high country for elk, but he had found nothing, not even sign. Suddenly, the Pale Man had appeared walking down a ridge toward him, right hand held high, palm out in the sign of peace. He was dressed only in a breechcloth and carried no weapons.

When he was about fifty paces from Many Moons, he stopped, and as the Indian watched, he pointed toward the east and the encampment of The People, one day hence. When Many Moons turned back from looking where he was pointing, the Pale Man had vanished.

Many Moons had started back to his village but had gone no more than a few hours travel when he found buffalo sign. A large herd had passed recently. Many

Moons followed the broad track until he located a valley that was filled with grazing buffalo. Now he could return to the village, gather the men, and return to this valley. The winter sustenance of The People was assured.

When he awoke from the dream, he puzzled over the meaning of this message and of the Pale Man. That summer the hunting was very good, and the tribe prospered.

Over the years, the Pale Man had appeared again and again, sometimes in dreams but more often when Many Moons had fasted for a proper vision, when seeking solution to problems facing the tribe. The Pale Man had always provided a sign that led Many Moons to a solution for the difficulty, so he had began to associate this strange figure with good tidings for The People. The Pale Man had never spoken to Many Moons, only signing in the universal language of the Indian.

Now Many Moons was seeing the reality of his dreams. The Pale Man was among them in the flesh. He seemed to be a good man, a warrior adept in arts that The People had never seen, arts that he was teaching to warriors of The People. Maybe his arrival was an indication of a war to come, and he was preparing The People, Many Moons conjectured. He would wait and see.

THE SHAMAN SPEAKS

Bryan was progressing at a rapid rate in his learning of the Tongue of The People. He was able to carry on a conversation, with only an occasional lapse into sign. White Bull seemed very pleased with his student, friend, and martial arts teacher. Their training classes had grown until they included most of the younger and some of the older warriors. The notable exceptions were the members of the Running Dog Lodge of Many Coups.

The shaman, Many Moons, sent word that he would like to have Bryan visit him, so Bryan went to his lodge and scratched on the door until he heard the invitation to enter.

The shaman bade him seat himself on the old man's right, a place of honor.

"You are becoming proficient in the Tongue," the old man stated. "It pleases me that I can now talk to you about what brings you to The People."

"I only wish that I could tell you," said Bryan. "But I know not myself. I awakened on a hillside, naked and unarmed three suns before I found your village."

"Maybe you will have a vision. Then you will learn what is the meaning of your visit," continued the Shaman. "I have known of your coming for many moons, and I can tell you something of this summons to The People."

Bryan was puzzled. "How were you told of my coming?" he asked.

The old man explained about his dreams and visions over the years and how they were directly related to the prosperity of The People. He explained how when The People sought advice or direction or help with difficult decisions, they fasted and prayed for a vision. He suggested that he and Bryan should fast together and seek the answer to their questions.

Bryan left the lodge after they exchanged polite pleasantries and returned to the lodge of White Bull, who had promised to help him make a war shield.

Bryan told White Bull of the questions posed by the shaman and the offer to fast and seek a vision together. White Bull was very impressed with this offer, which was unusual in that most visions were sought alone.

"I too have wondered why you are here," White Bull said. "But I thought that you would tell me when you were ready. Now I hear that you don't know yourself. The shaman is right. You should seek a vision."

The two men set about to make Bryan a shield. First, they obtained the hump skin of a buffalo from White Bull's store of hides. They cut a circle from the hide, half again bigger than the finished shield would be, and set the piece of hairless skin to soak in a vessel. Then they attached a limber, circular wooden frame and staked the hide over a small mound so that as the hide began to dry, it would take on a slightly convex shape. The finished, dried, hardened circular hide would be stitched to a frame with rawhide strips and then painted with the lodge totem of the bearer.

Throughout this process, Bryan was thinking about the shaman's words and his friend's concurrence.

"I should talk more to the Many Moons about this vision quest," he announced to White Bull that evening.

White Bull grunted in assent.

The next morning, after their training session, Bryan went to the lodge of the old shaman, made his presence known, and entered when bade to do so.

After seated and the polite pleasantries had been exchanged, Bryan got right to the point, a very non-Indian approach.

"Tell me how to go about this vision-quest, please."

The old man sat reflectively for a moment, then spoke, "First, you must prepare yourself in the sweat lodge and cleanse your body and system. I will have the preparations made when the signs are right. Since we do this together, I too must prepare. We will begin our fast after the sweat lodge, maybe by the new moon in one handful of suns."

All of Bryan's thoughts of the vision quest were put aside later that day when a party of hunters arrived with the news of the arrival of the first buffalo herds of the season. The village was in a hubbub of preparation for the great hunt on which their very existence depended.

THE BUFFALO HUNT

The very existence of The People depended upon the buffalo. From this animal they obtained meat; skins for tepees, robes and clothing; long hump hair was braided into ropes; bones were used for tools and implements; the stomachs were used for cooking and storage vessels; and the tails for fly whisks. In fact, The People had a saying that they "used everything on the buffalo but the bellow."

This great beast was revered to the point of worship. Buffalo horns were used for drinking cups or to adorn war bonnets. The buffalo dance was the center point of a ritual that both preceded the first hunt and celebrated the successes of it.

Without the mobility of the horse, which had yet to be introduced by the Spaniards to the New World, the hunting methods involved cooperation between all hunters. The herd had to be lured to a place where they could be driven over a cliff, or into a steep ravine, and the injured and trapped animals slaughtered. To do this was the task of the Buffalo Callers, warriors so skilled in deception. Dressed in hides of the buffaloes, they approached the herd, mingling with the outermost fringes, letting the animals become accustomed to their presence. Then, relying on the strong herding instinct, they gradually led the animals to the trap by pretending to graze in that direction. This usually took hours, sometimes days, and the success was a strong testimonial to the skill and patience of the Callers.

The balance of the hunters was arranged in a vee, the apex of which was the trap. When the herd entered the mouth of the vee, the outermost warriors arose from hiding and, with shouts and waving of shields and spears, moved the herd further into the vee, the mouth of the vee closing behind whatever portion of the herd which had entered. The panicked animals rushed into the trap, the first ones often fatally injuring themselves in the fall, the following ones becoming entrapped in the flailing bodies of their brothers. The warriors closed in and began to finish off the beasts.

The whole tribe was involved in the hunt and the butchering process, which was done on the spot due to the great bulk of the animals. Frequently, the heart and liver of the buffaloes were consumed raw, still warm and dripping blood. The animals were skinned, reduced to easily handled parcels, and then packed back to the village for the final processing. Dog-drawn travois were used to handle up to seventy-five pounds of meat, hide, and bones, and each person in the hunt—warriors, women, and even children—shouldered sizable packs for transport. Usually, the only signs of the hunt that remained at the site were the bloody patches where the beasts were butchered. Everything else was transported to the village for use by The People.

Bryan got caught up in the excitement of the preparation. Following White Bull's lead, he gathered his lance, which the brave had helped him make by donating a long, flint point, helping select the shaft and fastening the head, and the new shield they had made. They were to be part of the mouth of the trap.

Faces West called the tribe together to outline the plan for the hunt. Since the herd was close by, it would not be necessary to move the village closer, a lucky and unusual circumstance. The killing ground would be a deep draw between the herd and the village. The Buffalo Callers, all older and experienced hunters, were dispatched, and then the rest of the tribe was divided into two parties, one under Faces West and the other under another senior warrior, each of whom would place his charges into the legs of the vee. Only a smattering of old people and children would be left in the village because this was the critical hunting season for all tribes and there was little likelihood of an raid by their enemies.

Bryan was in the party led by Faces West, along with White Bull and many of the young warriors from the training class. The chief placed them about twenty-five or thirty yards apart until they had a line that stretched nearly half a mile from the ravine. The other leader did the same with his group, and the end hunters in each group were nearly a half mile apart, forming two sides of a nearly equilateral triangle, the mouth of the trap being the third side, leaving a small opening about fifty yards wide at the ravine. Then they settled down for the long wait.

The site of the hunt was slightly undulating prairie covered with knee-high grass. Each hunter in the vee sought a place of concealment, a hummock of grass or the rare bush or often a small depression into which they could crouch. The day was warming up as the sun rose in the sky. The only sounds were birds and insects. Hours passed and Bryan found himself getting drowsy in the warmth of the spring sun. His mind drifted aimlessly as he half-dozed. He was the fourth man from the mouth of the vee, White Bull on his left, closer to the opening, and another man to his right, but he could see neither in their concealment.

He became aware of distant sounds and became alert. The noises increased until he could hear the grunting and rumbling of the buffaloes. He risked a peek, but a small rise in front prevented him from seeing anything. Soon though, he could hear the outermost hunters begin to make noise as they rose and began to shout and bang their lances against their shields and circle behind the group of animals that had entered the mouth of the vee. When he heard White Bull's voice raised in a shout, Bryan arose from his concealment and moved to the top of the rise a few yards in front.

The sight that greeted him was roiling in dust amongst which he could see the panicking buffaloes beginning to lope toward the trap. He began to join in the shouting and banging, and soon, he heard the man on his right join in too. The group of animals began to pass, and Bryan moved to join the line pushing the beasts toward the killing ground. The buffaloes were now in a full stampede, about a hundred of them, bearing down on the ravine. Occasionally, one of them would attempt to veer off, but the line of shouting, noisy hunters kept most of them from escaping.

Following the leaders, the animals plunged into the ravine, the first ones being crushed under the weight of those immediately behind them, all of them being pushed into the trap by the weight of the rushing herd following.

Bryan moved in with the rest of the hunters but was not being quite sure how to kill one of the beasts, so he contented himself with helping White Bull dispatch several by jabbing with his spear to distract the animal while the Indian struck at vital areas. In what seemed like almost no time, it was over. Warriors moved among the downed animals, finishing off any which still moved. About fifty of the herd had been killed in the trap. The others, having either made it through the lines of warriors or being behind the leaders, were able to cross the ravine over the bodies of the others and escape.

The butchering and packing of the spoils back to the village took the remainder of the day and well into the next day before it was done. In all, it had been a successful hunt. The final processing into dried meat, pemmican, tools, and tanned hides would begin, but first, there was to be a celebration.

THE FEAST

The day after the successful buffalo hunt was spent in preparing the meat for preservation. Strips of the loins, hams, and briskets were put on high racks for drying. After which, much of it would be pounded with berries and animal fat, then wrapped in wet hide pouches, which, when dried, would compress the compound into hard blocks—pemmican, the winter diet staple of the People.

The organs, including the tongues, hearts, and livers, were set aside for the coming celebration, along with the hump, tenderloin, and rib meat. The stomachs were set aside for fashioning into cooking and storage vessels while the intestines were hung on sticks over the cooking fires for immediate consumption while The People worked over the results of their hunt. This *boudin*, as the French trappers and mountain men of a later era called it, was a delicacy in the eyes of The People.

The hides were pegged out for scraping and curing. The women used bone and stone scrapers to remove any fat and tissue from the hides. The continued scraping would soften the skin somewhat and prepare it for the tanning process, which was accomplished by continuous rubbing with a mixture of the animal's brains, stomach gall, and urine. The more this was rubbed into the hide, the softer it became. The buffalo had not yet completely lost their winter coats, so the hair on the hides was still thick. The later, summer hides were usually reserved for tepee skins from which it was easier to remove the hair.

The bones of the beasts were saved to dry out and fashion into tools, weapons, needles, and containers. The hoofs were used to make glue for laminating bows and shields.

As evening drew near, the women set about preparing the feast of celebration. The cooking fires were heaped with wood and buffalo "chips" and spitted meat placed over them, along side were placed the cooking vessels into which were poured odds and ends of meat, organs, water, herbs, and tubers for a savory stew, which was cooked by hot rocks from the cooking fire. In short order, the delicious aroma of cooking meat permeated the camp.

Bryan and White Bull dressed in their finery, Bryan having been supplied with quill decorated buckskin shirts, leggings, and moccasins by some of his students out of appreciation for the lessons while the White Bull's mother and sister prepared their dishes in front of the lodge. Each family group was cooking, and it was expected that everyone would visit as many lodges as possible to sample their offerings.

Bryan and White Bull began to circulate through the camp, stopping and eating at the lodges of friends, students, the chief... Bryan ate sparingly to avoid stuffing himself too early, but he noticed that White Bull was not so judicious. As the evening wore on, Bryan became very full, but the Indian continued to eat at each tepee where they stopped. Bryan was amazed at his capacity and began to notice that the other men were also eating prodigious amounts. Apparently, their stomachs were much more flexible than his because if White Bull was any indication, they could eat two or three times as much as Bryan.

They were greeted with great courtesy at each lodge, and there were stories told and much friendly laughter everywhere. Each brave recounted his version of the hunt and his exploits to the audience at every stop, the stories growing with each telling. Bryan figured that if all the stories that he heard were accurate, and then there must have been several hundred buffaloes killed, not fifty or so. *Hunters are no different at any period through the ages*, he thought, recalling all the tales told at hunting camps in his "other" life.

Finally, groaning with distended stomachs, everyone retreated to their respective lodges and fell into their sleeping robes.

The following day, the feast continued with the day filled with games and contests. The People were very competitive and loved to stage footraces, target matches with bows, spears, and throwing sticks, wrestling matches and games of chance using dice made from buffalo bones.

At White Bull's urging, Bryan staged a karate demonstration. He first had all students line up and put them through all their basic techniques—blocks, punches and kicks. Then, they formed into two opposing lines and demonstrated *ippon kumite*, one-step sparing in which one person attacked with a single technique while the other blocked the attack and countered with their own attack. The purpose of the drill in training is to condition the reflexes to respond appropriately to any type of attack, whether punches, kicks, or from a weapon.

The natural affinity of the Indians to use their voices in warfare lead to their easy assumption of the *kiai*, the explosion of noise used in martial arts techniques to freeze an opponent and to add force to their offensive punches and kicks. Bryan knew how impressive it must look and sound to the onlookers as the class went through the drills in unison, their loud *kiais* resounding.

Bryan had several pairs of the more adept trainees spar, freestyle, with light contact. It was very apparent to the onlookers when a blow or kick would have been crippling if the technique had not been pulled. A low "huh" from the onlookers greeted every telling kick or blow.

The festivities were interrupted by excited cries from the outskirts of the camp. The ever-present sentinels had spotted the returning war party of Many Coups. They had been gone nearly ten days and had missed the great hunt. As they strode toward the center of the camp, a noisy crowd, who were exclaiming over their trophies of the raid, the most notable of which was a young Pawnee woman on a tether behind Many Coups, surrounded them.

The warriors had painted themselves for their triumphant return and were decked out in their finery, coup feathers, quill decorated shirts, and leggings, their best moccasins and each with their personal paint patterns in black, white, ochre, or yellow. Their arrival at the height of the festivities could not have been timed better.

THE RAID

Many Coups did not just plan a raid and then execute the plan. In the way of The People, there was a mystical significance to everything. He had "dreamed" of the raid, so therefore, he had begun to plan one.

Normally, he would have first he had gone to the old shaman, Many Moons, to ask for a sign or vision for his plans. While awaiting the response, he and the members of the Running Dog Society would cleanse themselves in the sweat lodge and fasted for a day until the shaman had summoned Many Coups to his lodge. The disapproval of Faces West, the chief, precluded him from seeking help from the shaman, so he made preparations on his own.

Many Coups saw no hazards for the raid; in fact, he had seen a successful conclusion for the effort. Negative signs would not necessarily abort the mission but would have given a warning of what to guard against. Only if the omens were totally negative would the raid be canceled or postponed.

Six warriors left just after dusk, traveling in familiar surroundings in the dark so that their departure would go unnoticed by any enemy who might be scouting their camp. After several hours of stealthy travel, they sought shelter among the willows in a creek bottom, where they rested until just before first light. They left the draw, single file, chewing on their breakfast of jerky.

They traveled light, carrying only their weapons and a small pouch containing jerky, containers of paint, and a medicine bag to ward off spirits. Each warrior carried a flint knife in a scabbard thrust through his belt, a short war spear, and slung across his back was his bow case and quiver of flint-tipped arrows. Their pace was a ground-consuming dogtrot to the northwest, toward the hunting ground of their traditional enemies, the Pawnee. It was the hope of Many Coups to come across the village there had been signs of before many days travel, reconnoiter the camp, then stage a stealthy foray, coming away with some booty and having counted coup on their enemy, maybe even taking a captive if the opportunity presented itself.

The purpose of the raiding amongst the tribes was not so much to kill their enemy as it was to demonstrate the bravery of the warriors by counting coup, touching an enemy without harming them, coming away unharmed, and taking valuables and captives. The latter were usually kept as slaves though many of them were often assimilated into the tribe through marriage or by their personal bravery.

Most warlike encounters between Native American tribes was in the form of small raids, like this one of Many Coups', very seldom escalating to armed conflict between large groups or prolonged campaigns.

After two days of travel, the band came to the area where the Pawnee village had been seen. While the group rested in a draw, Many Coups scouted ahead and located the village, which he spied upon from concealment on a brushy hillside.

There were only ten lodges in the camp, meaning probably no more than thirty warriors or less. Only in war camps were there more men of warrior status, often as many as five to a lodge, and this appeared to be a simple early summer hunting encampment of a Pawnee clan. The activity around the camp appeared normal, the people unalarmed and not aware of the enemy presence. After watching for much of the afternoon, Many Coups returned to his party in the draw.

Stealth, rather than a noisy entry into the camp, was the normal plan. Early the next morning, the Running Dog soldiers crept through the gloom, into the Pawnee camp, going in pairs to the lodges indicated by Many Coups as those most likely to contain easily carried booty. Quietly they took weapons and tools from outside racks, as well as some dried meat, being sure to leave obvious signs that they had been there. Their concentration was on lodges in the center of the village to show their bravery, but when they passed out, they paused at two lodges on the perimeter where the entrance flaps were pulled back to allow Many Coups and another to enter and strike the occupants with their coup sticks and depart quickly, whooping, leaving the rudely awakened people stunned into inactivity.

The whooping Cheyenne fled the camp, leaving rising sounds of alarm in their wake. They knew that it would be a few minutes before the Pawnee would be able to sort out the hubbub and mount a pursuit. They would not be sure how many were in the attacking party, and it would take time to assemble a large-enough group to feel safe enough to venture out of the village. Sometimes these night forays were used to draw the enemy into a trap by larger war parties.

While fleeing toward the brushy hillside, they surprised a young woman who had left the lodge, probably to relieve herself, and binding her hands in front with tough rawhide rope, they attached a tether around her neck and continued their flight. The woman did not resist greatly because she knew that it could result in her death if she impeded their escape. She would have to await a better opportunity to escape from what she recognized as "cut-fingers" or Cheyenne.

After they had fled north out of the Pawnee village, they turned east, taking care to erase their signs in order to delay pursuit. Several hours later, they turned southeast, back toward their own village. Their travel was slowed considerably due to the care with which they covered the signs of their passage. They knew that the Pawnee would by now know who had perpetrated the attack, and soon, the war party would have to be alert for possible ambush, for though they had been careful to circle the camp and approach from a different direction than they had arrived from, the Pawnee might have sent pursuit toward the Cheyenne country rather than to try and track the small war party.

To prevent ambush, Many Coups sent a scout ahead, and they changed directions several times each hour to confuse any trackers. They had come far enough now not to worry about sign, so they picked up the pace to a trot.

Many Coups had a chance to look over his captive now. She was a comely maid in her late teens, dressed only in a calf-length buckskin dress and moccasins. Her ebony hair had been loosened for the night and fell about her shoulders. During one of their pauses, she had quickly braided it into a single strand, tying the end with a bit of rawhide thong, torn from a seam of her dress. She was unable to do more because of her tied hands and the shortness of their stop. Many Coups took notice of the girl's efforts and thought to himself that it spoke well of her spirit to not be so numbed by her capture that she did not take care of herself. The braid that hung down her back would not catch in the brush or hinder her travel as much as free-swinging long tresses.

The route set by Many Coups carried the war party to the north of their village, to further throw off any pursuers who might come this far. Then, they turned south into their home ground. In all, they had been gone nearly ten days when they came close to their village.

The group paused a few hours from their home to prepare for their entry. They renewed their paint, put on their finery, and broke out the booty before entering the village. Many Coups took note of the celebration in progress and was pleased with the timing of their return.

THE PAWNEE GIRL SPEAKS

She Who Talks Fast had known eighteen summers but was still unmarried. She was tall, willowy, and pretty, but her band of Pawnees was small, with few marriageable young men, and she did not want to be a second wife to an older one, so she discouraged their interest by chattering a lot when she knew a seasoned warrior was looking her over. Their band usually hunted the outer reaches of the traditionally tribal hunting grounds, so there was less contact with other bands where there might have been more young men.

She had been restless and had risen, gone to the bushes to relieve herself when the Cheyenne braves had taken her. During the trek back to her village, she had watched for a chance to escape but found her captors vigilant, and no opportunity was presented. She was a hardy girl, with a strong will, so she was not overly depressed by her capture. In fact, she had examined these Cheyenne braves and found them young and attractive, particularly her guard, who seemed to be the leader, so she was optimistic that she could make the best of the situation.

After several days' travel, they arrived at the village of the "cut-fingers," as the Cheyenne were known to the other Plains tribes because of their habit of cutting off the fingers, or even hands, of their fallen enemies.

Talks Fast found herself the center of attention as the little group made their way to the center of the village. The signs of the successful hunt were evident by the meat-filled racks and the festive atmosphere of the people. She understood a little of the Cheyenne tongue, and she confirmed that her captor, Many Coups, was a highly regarded warrior. She saw no young woman greet him, so she assumed that he was unmarried. Her fertile mind worked on this for a minute.

She looked around at the villagers as Many Coups recounted the tale of their raid. The men were showing off their captured weapons and other items to the admiring crowd. There would be a formal storytelling later, but the young men could not help but to boast a little.

Suddenly, Talks Fast was stunned. There was a tall, pale man with much facial hair standing in the crowd. Although he was dressed as a Cheyenne, he was obviously of a different people. She recalled having heard of a Pale Man living with another band of Pawnee but had discounted this as being just a light-skinned Indian, but now she could see that this man here was not of any tribe she had ever seen or heard of, so maybe, the one among the Pawnee was of the same tribe as this one.

Many Coups saw the girl's interest in the Pale Man and spoke, "Do not fear the Pale Man, Pawnee woman.

You are in the custody of the Running Dog Lodge and need not fear anything from him."

"I do not fear him," she replied in halting Cheyenne. "I have heard of one like him amongst my people, a clan in the far west of our hunting ground, but I have never seen him. This one is so pale and looks strange with the hair on his face."

Many Coups was startled. "You have heard of another Pale Man?"

"For many moons now, there has been told of one like him." She inclined her head toward Bryan. "He lives with the Black Wolf band in the high country to the west."

Later, in conference with Faces West, Many Coups recounted what the Pawnee captive had told him. Faces West too was startled and told his young brave that the captive should be brought to be questioned by Many Moons and him.

While awaiting the girl, he went to Many Moons's lodge and told him of what he heard.

When the girl was ushered into the lodge, Faces West, without the formality reserved for men, bade her be seated. She had been briefed by Many Coups and began to respond immediately when questioned by the chief about a pale man among the Pawnee.

"For several moons now," she began, "there have been stories brought by travelers amongst our people about a pale skinned man living with the Black Wolf band in the West. Many of us thought that he was just a light-skinned Indian from another tribe, but now that I have seen your Pale Man, I do not know. They must be from the same tribe."

"How long has he been with the Black Wolves?" asked Faces West.

"I do not know. We only started to hear of him during the past few moons, maybe since we moved out of our winter camp, but he could have been with them for many moons."

The Pawnee woman told of how the stories came to her clan by way of passing hunters and travelers between bands, of a pale man who had come to them, naked and unarmed and was now living with the Pawnee. There was little else to tell.

The chief dismissed the girl and Many Coups. He was concerned about what they had learned.

"What do you make of this tale?" he said to Many Moons. The old shaman had remained silent during the questioning.

"Maybe we have a new tribe on the plains. I have heard of the Mandan people on the great river to the north. They are said to be pale skinned, but our Pale Man has said that he is from another place altogether. Maybe this Pawnee pale man is of his tribe. We should ask him."

THE VISION QUEST

Bryan answered the summons to the lodge of Many Moons where he found the old shaman and the chief awaiting him. When he was seated across from them and the formalities were over, the shaman spoke.

"The Pawnee girl has said that there is another pale man like you Bry-Yan. He is living among their people in a western band, near the Mountains of the Clouds."

Bryan was stunned. "I do not know how I came to be among the people, but if I came here, then someone else could have also." He paused. "How long has this person been among the Pawnee?"

"The girl did not know, but she said that they have been hearing stories of his presence for several moons now. Nothing before that," replied the shaman.

"That is how long I have been with The People," Bryan said. "Maybe whatever brought me here also brought others, but how...and why?" he mused aloud.

"Maybe it is your destiny," said Many Moons. "You and I should seek a vision which will answer these questions. We will purify ourselves by fasting and in the sweat lodge, then retire to a dreaming place."

Preparations were made for the purification. The sweat lodge fire was stoked to a blaze and round rocks placed in the perimeter to heat and a large vessel of water was placed by the fire. Bryan and the shaman entered the small, nearly airtight, round roofed lodge, only a smoke hole penetrating the envelope after the small entrance flap was fastened behind them. They had stripped to a breechcloth before entering and were now seated on the hard ground.

Many Moons maneuvered a rock to the edge of the water vessel with two forked sticks and dropped it in. A loud hissing, then steam began to fill the top of the lodge. Another rock, more hissing, and the steam began to thicken. Bryan could barely see the old man now. He felt the sweat begin to breakout all over his body, running off his face and dripping into his lap. The air got so thick and wet it was difficult to breathe. Bryan kept his head down and breathed shallowly. The air was very hot in his lungs. He had been in steam baths and saunas before, but this was the hottest. He did not know how long he could stay in the lodge but vowed not to leave until the old man did.

It seemed to go on for hours. Frequently, the old shaman would remove the cooling rocks from the water and replace them with hot ones from the fire. The air was still hot and damp, but Bryan could feel himself getting used to it. He tried Zen meditation he learned in his martial arts training and found that he could remove himself from the discomfort. The sweat continued to pour off his body, soaking the breechcloth and the ground around him. He could not see him clearly, but the shaman seemed to be meditating, rocking slightly to and fro. Bryan withdrew into his own meditation.

His mind returned to the present when the shaman began a low, guttural chant. He seemed to be asking the spirits for guidance in the matter of the pale men. What did their presence mean to The People?

After what seemed like several hours, the shaman laboriously rose and opened the sweat lodge entrance flap. Bryan followed him out, then down to the stream flowing nearby, where they immersed themselves in the cool water. Bryan expected a shock but was surprised at the balmy effect of the water. After a few minutes, they rose from the stream and started back to the shaman's lodge.

The old man broke the silence. "We have purified our bodies. Now we will retire to the dream place and pray for a vision."

They each gathered a small robe, shirt, and leggings and headed out of the village into a rocky draw nearby. Following the old man, Bryan picked his way among the rocks, noticing that they were heading for a high ledge in the small canyon.

Upon arrival at the ledge, Bryan followed the old man's lead and spread his robe on the flat rocky space, clearing any small stones from the area. The shaman directed Bryan to be seated alongside him, facing the east. The old man closed his eyes and began his low chanting prayer for a vision. Bryan closed his eyes also and began to meditate.

Bryan's first karate instructor was an American who had learned his art in the Orient from old masters who did not neglect the Zen side of his training, as is often the case in the United States. Thus, Bryan had an appreciation of the power of the mind and a trained person's ability to focus himself through meditation. He knew of cases of accelerated healing of minor injuries, and he had often used Zen to review his techniques and forms when he was not in a position to practice physically.

From reading Dr. Maxwell Maltz's *Psycho Cybernetics*, Bryan knew of experiments with control groups where half the group practiced a physical exercise, the other half thought about it, and both groups improved their performance equally, advancing the theory that athletic practice is as much for mind/body coordination as it is for physical conditioning. Dr. Max theorized that the mind was a programmable machine, much like a computer, and we are capable of doing the programming ourselves. Bryan began to meditate for a vision, alongside the old shaman.

They had brought no food since fasting was part of the purification of their bodies, but they had brought water bags from which they took an occasional sip. As the day wore on, Bryan became oblivious to the discomforts of his body—the hard ground, his rumbling stomach, and giddiness from the effects of it all. He was reaching a state of mental concentration, the likes of which he had never experienced. He was dimly aware that Many Moons was in a trance-like state, occasionally muttering a chant or prayer to the spirits he was trying to reach.

Bryan began to have random thoughts about his past life. He reflected back on his early days...his parents...his friends...his start in the martial arts. His mind scrolled past his education and how he had gone into teaching, more from a lack of knowing what he wanted than from a specific purpose. He reviewed briefly all of the things that he had experienced: college, ROTC, the army and his ranger training, karate, and paint-ball gun battles with his friends during and after his military career. All of the time, he had been seeking purpose...a reason for being, without being conscious of this. He reveled in the physical challenges.

Bryan's meditation moved to the present. The People, White Bull, and the others in the training class, Strong Woman... Ah, he could see her in his mind as he had so often watched with his eyes. The graceful way she moved, her flanks flexing under her buckskin skirt when she walked, her dark beauty, ebony hair... She filled his mind. His meditation deepened. He became aware of the old man, his mind seeking answers to the puzzles of life, looking for guidance to deal with Bryan's presence and now that of another pale man. The shaman was motivated only by his desire to know and how it affected The People. He had only their best interests in mind, not to advance any personal agenda.

Bryan began to see with great clarity that he would have to seek the answers to the questions posed by his presence among The People and in this land. He had been diverted by the plethora of new experiences over the past weeks and had lost sight of what should have been his real goal...to find out where he was and, most importantly, why he was here!

The sun had sunk into the western sky, and long shadows marked the end of the day, but still the two men sat on the remote ledge. The old man surfaced from his trance, and Bryan too was back inside his own skin.

The shaman spoke, his voice hoarse from all of the chanting, "I have not seen clearly yet. The spirits are trying to reach me, but I have not been able to hear them." He drank sparingly from a water bag. "There is a reason for your coming among The People, that much I am sure of. It may be to fulfill your destiny, or it may be to bring about some change in ours. We must continue to quest."

Bryan nodded his assent. He had not experienced anything he could interpret as a vision, only his life in review, so he had nothing to contribute.

They got up and moved around the ledge to restore their circulation. Bryan did some pre-training stretching to loosen up, drank some water, and returned to his seated position, alongside the old man, who had watched the routine with interest.

"Maybe you have come to teach The People a new art of war," Many Moons uttered reflectively. "It could be that your destiny is linked to The People, and you will prepare us to defend against our enemies."

The day had completely fled now, and the darkness closed in around them, almost as a physical presence. They returned to their meditation, the shaman chanting quietly for his vision.

Renewed by the brief respite, Bryan focused inwardly and soon felt himself begin to lose awareness of his physical being. Again, his mind sought answers and what he got was a more detailed examination of the past. To bring himself back to the present, he began to perform kata in his mind, beginning with the most basic forms.

How much time passed, he did not know, but Bryan became aware he had been sleeping. He was awake now, but he was not on the ledge but rather on a plain. He was among his training class of Cheyenne braves, and they were all painted for war. He was conscious of a threat from the west. What type of danger, he knew not, only that it was there, just over the horizon.

White Bull was at his shoulder as the group strode toward the dim horizon, and no one was saying anything. As they walked purposefully west, the distance did not seem to shorten as if they were on a treadmill.

Bryan became aware that their group was growing in numbers. There was Strong Woman at his other shoulder, Faces West beside her, and old Many Moons striding along on youthful legs. He glanced around and saw that the entire clan was trekking west with him, even Many Coups and his Running Dog Lodge brothers. All of them seemed intent on something over the horizon, but the feeling of threat, danger, had diminished...

He became aware that he was back on the ledge. He opened his eyes and found the shaman staring fixedly at him.

"I guess I was asleep," he stammered. "I was dreaming..."

"You had a vision," said the old man. "Tell me about your dream. Maybe I can help you understand what the spirits are telling you."

Bryan recounted his experience, all of it being very fresh in his mind, not at all like a dream which vanishes upon awaking, leaving only a vague memory. The details were clear as he spoke.

The shaman sat reflectively for a while, thinking about what he had heard. Then he offered his thoughts.

"I think that the spirits are telling you that you are here to influence the destiny of The People. You are to nullify a threat to us from the west, but your destiny does not stop here. You will then leave us and seek the answers to all of your questions, probably traveling to the west. You will not go alone. The heart of The People will go with you, but you will have companions too. Their identities will be revealed to you...or to them!"

Many Moons continued, "I too have had a vision. I was visited by the Sun who told me that I was to prepare you to fulfill your vision by teaching you the history of The People, so you will better understand how you must help us." He went on, "The Sun told me that there is a great shaman among the Mountain People, the Paiutes, who will provide the answers you seek, if you find that you still want them. All of this will come later. How much later, I was not told."

They sat on the ledge until the light began to streak the eastern sky, Many Moons telling of the history of his tribe through their myths and legends and of their trek from their original homeland far to the northeast in the lake country.

BRYAN AND STRONG WOMAN

Bryan and Many Moons returned to the village shortly after sunrise, and at the old man's suggestion, they stopped at his lodge where he went in, coming out in a moment with a roll of buckskin.

"I have had this for many years. I got it from an Omaha who had traded for it from the Metalworkers by the Great Water," he said, opening the bundle. Inside was a knife made from what appeared to be copper. The handle was of some hard wood, possibly ash or maple, darkened by the sweat of many years of handling. The blade was broad and thick but tapered nicely near the edge. Hammer marks were visible, and so it had probably been fashioned from a nugget of pure, unsmelted copper. The craftsmanship was very good.

"This is my gift to you," said the shaman.

Bryan didn't know what to say. He just took the blade and looked at it, turning it this way and that. There seemed to be a fairly good edge on it. Copper, being fairly soft, was easily worked and would take an edge but would not hold it well.

"I will always honor this gift," Bryan finally said. The old man smiled, patted his shoulder, and returned to his tepee, leaving Bryan standing there.

When he got back to White Bull's lodge, he got a piece of stiff buffalo hide and tried stropping the blade. After a time, he found that he had put a very good edge on the knife, trying it on his arm hair. He was pleased to see it shave cleanly. He tried it on his face but found that it pulled too much to shave his beard cleanly. Removing the growth of months was going to take lather.

He thought back to ranger survival training, his Army Field Manual section on hygiene. The elements were present. He only had to put them together... He could make soap!

The Cheyenne, like most Indians, are a very clean people. They value personal cleanliness greatly, using ashes or sand as cleansers for most things. On occasion, they use the Agave plant, a source of a soap-like sap, which is a good cleaner, but they do not have anything that will provide the lather necessary to shave a heavy beard.

From Strong Woman, Bryan secured some animal fat, which he placed in a hide vessel by the cooking fire, close enough to melt the fat, into which he poured some water to keep it from sticking as it cooked. He stirred frequently until the fat was rendered, then poured it into another container to harden. He then collected a quantity of ashes and mixed it into a slurry with water, then carefully pouring off the liquid, holding the ashes back with his hand. The resulting liquid is potash or lye.

Bryan then put two parts of his rendered fat and one part potash in his vessel and cooked it until it had thickened. He removed it from the heat and let it cool. The resulting mixture was a rude, but effective, soap. While it was still soft enough to pour, he spread it in a long, narrow line on a strip of hide and allowed it to harden completely, then cut it into bars.

He could hardly wait to try it. Taking a bar of soap and his copper knife, he went to the stream, going a little downstream from the camp so as not to be observed. He stripped and got into a small pool at the base of a creek willow. The soap worked effectively. The stream water was soft enough for it to produce a good lather with which he thoroughly washed his hair and beard. He worked up a second lather in his beard and then began to carefully shave away the tangled growth. In short order, he was relatively clean cheeked. The knife had begun to dull toward the last, but a few strops on the leather put the edge back on enough to finish.

Back at the lodge, his clean-cut appearance brought exclamations of surprise from Strong Woman and her mother. White Bull just smiled knowingly at Bryan. Both of the women had to run their hands over his smooth face, plying him with questions.

Bryan showed them the soap he had made, explaining how he had done it. Then he showed the blade given him by the shaman and explained that in his land, most of the men shaved their faces every day and now that he had the means, he expected to do the same.

Later, White Bull commented, "I am glad that you took off your facial hair. Few of our people have any. Those who do have so little that they pluck it out. Our slaves are not allowed to remove the hair. It is a sign of servitude, but they immediately do so if they are adopted into The People. No one would have thought of you as a slave, but I am still glad to see the hair gone." The Cheyenne smiled slyly. "I am sure that my sister is also glad to see it gone." Bryan blushed at the thought of Strong Woman caring about his appearance.

Ever since his arrival at their lodge, Bryan was very aware of Strong Woman. At first, he had assumed that she was White Bull's wife and avoided looking too closely, but after his language skills had improved enough for them to converse, he learned from White Bull that she was his sister, Strong Woman.

Her name, Bryan learned, had been derived from her strength of character and strong, obstinate will. She was very competitive and had sharp tongue when crossed. These very unmaidenly ways had kept a line from forming at the lodge door when she reached marriage age, but her father had delighted in his strong-willed daughter and catered to her whims though not excessively so.

Her physical beauty still attracted those who thought they might tame this wild creature, but she showed little interest in most of them. Lately, Many Coups had begun to show interest in her, and she was somewhat receptive, being encouraged to show respect to him by her mother, who was worried about her "old maid" daughter.

Bryan had begun to watch her covertly. She handled tasks easily and cheerfully, never shirking her duties. She was usually the first to stir up the morning fire for food preparation, and she prepared the majority of the meals. She was always active, keeping busy at every waking hour. She always finished the household tasks early so she could do the other things that interested her. Her particular delight was in her decorative work on clothing and painting the story of her family on the lodge hides. She even went so far as to help paint White Bull and Bryan's shields, a warrior's duty, but one that they allowed her to do because of her talent and they knew it would please her. A pleased Strong Woman was a joy to have around. On the other hand...

Strong Woman was very much aware of Bryan and his watching her. She was very impressed by his physical appearance, but there had been other big, strong men who had shown interest but could not cope with her spirit, so they moved on to more submissive women. *This one is different*, she thought, *and he comes from a far place and will probably want to return*. However, as time passed and Bryan got more involved in activities with her brother and the training class he established, she began to think that he might stay with The People, and she started to think differently of him.

In Bryan's world, he had always been respectful of women. He had been exposed to a number of independent women, beginning with his mother and an aunt, his father's sister, and he had learned that they only sought respect for their abilities and contributions and did not want to be deferred to because they were female. He recognized this same attitude in Strong Woman and was not put off by it. In fact, he appreciated it. Most of the girls he had been attracted to over the years were strong, talented people.

In time, Bryan got over his initial shyness and began to talk to Strong Woman. He praised her artistic efforts in a non patronizing manner and talked to her about how to tan hides, prepare pemmican, erect a lodge, and many other everyday activities among The People. He wanted to get to know her, but also he was interested in their way of life.

Occasionally, at night, he caught further glimpses of her, partially nude, which only contributed to greater interest in her. His initial attraction was physical. She was an attractive, sensuous, woman, but as they became better acquainted, he was drawn to her intelligence, wit, and talents.

Bryan was not sure how to go about pursuing this Cheyenne woman. He didn't want to make a faux pas, but his attraction and need was so strong that he had to do something.

One day, while he and White Bull were resting during a one-on-one karate training session, he said, "There is something I need to ask you, but I do not want to offend."

"You may speak to me of anything, my brother," replied the brave.

"It is about your sister. I find her very attractive, but I do not know how to tell her so. I am not familiar enough with your customs, and I do not want to offend her," said Bryan. "Or you or her mother," he added.

"You can show your interest in several ways," offered White Bull. "You can use an intermediary to tell her of your interest." White Bull smiled. "I might consider to undertake this. Or you can approach the head of her family...me, with gifts to show your intent is honorable."

"What types of gifts?" asked Bryan.

"A shield, weapons, buffalo robes, or other animal skins... Anything of value which you have or can make," continued the Cheyenne. "Since you are so new among The People and have not accumulated many possessions, there are other things you can do, like provide a service like karate training or soap making or something like that." The Indian was now grinning broadly, and Bryan began to realize that his friend was pleased at Bryan's interest in his sister and not teasing him.

"Bry-Yan, I think that you will find your attraction is not unacceptable to Strong Woman. I will mention it to her on your behalf," continued Strong Bull, a little more seriously.

Later, Bryan found that Strong Woman was looking at him a little differently when they talked, and he realized that his friend's estimate of her interest was correct. She was indeed receptive to his attentions, but he was not quite sure how to proceed. He was living in her brother and mother's lodge, and he had no place to take her. It wasn't as if he could ask her out on a date. His immediate answer was to spend more time with this beautiful woman, and maybe the chance would present itself for him to advance their relationship to the next step.

STRONG WOMAN
MAKES THE MOVE

Strong Woman was very pleased when her brother told her of Bry-Yan's interest in her. She had been afraid that her independence would scare him off as it had a number of others, and she was very attracted to him physically and because of the way he treated her as an equal. She tried to send the signals to him for him to make the next move, signals that any Cheyenne brave would understand, but he paid them no attention. She guessed that these things were done differently in his land, so she decided that the next move was up to her, if their relationship was to grow into what she hoped it would.

She was very much aware that Bry-Yan had a regular schedule. After the morning training session, which she watched covertly, the pale man would generally talk at length with the old shaman, Many Moons, hearing of the origins and legends of The People and telling a little of his world. Then he would sometimes meet with Faces West, the chief with whom he exchanged ideas on training and governing a group of independent individuals. But usually, he went out of the village to practice alone the skills he was learning from White Bull on tracking, hunting, and weaponry.

This day, she watched carefully his morning schedule; and when she saw him leave the village, she noted his direction of travel. When several hours had passed, his usual length of absence, she went to a pool in the creek, upstream from the camp, where he would pass on his return to the village. Undressing, she took one of the bars of soap Bry-Yan had made, immersed herself in the water, and began to bathe herself leisurely, starting with her raven hair.

She did not splash around and make much noise, so she could hear his footfalls as he returned. When she heard the faint sounds of his passage through the trees along the creek bank, she began to make a little noise, splashing and humming to herself, and moved into the shallows of the pool where she stood in the thigh-deep water, rinsing the soap from her body, when he appeared on the near bank.

Strong Woman turned and saw him standing there, mouth agape and a look on his face that was so funny she almost laughed aloud. She moved toward the bank, got out, went to his side, and looked up at him.

He was still speechless, so she asked, "Does it please Bry-Yan to look upon me?"

He stammered what sounded like a positive response, so she continued, "It pleases me that you like to look at me. I want to look good for you so that you will want to hold me."

He needed no more encouragement than that and took her in his arms, holding her close for a moment before he placed his mouth on hers. This was a strange move. The People did not touch mouths, and at first, she did not know what to make of it, but soon, she felt her passions rise and began to return the kiss. Her mouth parted slightly, and she felt his tongue exploring the tip of hers, and a tingling spread from her innermost parts throughout her body. She pulled him to where she had laid her clothes on a robe, brought in anticipation, and they eased down on it, still kissing and touching each other.

They lay there in each other's arms for what seemed like hours. Bry-Yan looked into her eyes and said something in his native tongue. She did not understand the words but knew their meaning because of what she was feeling for him.

MANY COUPS MOVES AGAINST BRYAN

Many Coups was incensed. This pale man, this interloper, had humiliated him in front of his lodge, had developed a clan group of his own along with White Buffalo, was becoming a confidant of the old shaman and the chief, and now, adding insult to injury, he was romantically involved with the woman Many Coups had designs on.

In the days following Bryan and Strong Woman's first tryst, it became obvious to all observers what had happened. When the two lovers were together, they had eyes for no one else. Many Coups had seen them and knew he had lost again, and he had not ever lost until the pale man came on the scene. It was time to do something about it!

He set out on a subtle whisper campaign, uttering questioning statements about Bry-Yan, whenever the pale man's name came up in conversations with other warriors, statements aimed at casting doubt on the purpose of his presence with The People. What was he doing here? What were his aims? Where were his people?

As time passed, Many Coups increased the vehemence of his statements, now taking an accusatory tone. Is this pale one a spy? Is he here to learn of our weaknesses so he can lead his own people against us?

Bryan was so caught up in Strong Woman that he did not hear the undercurrent of suspicion that his enemy was creating, but White Bull did.

"Bry-Yan," he said, "It pleases me to see what has happened between my sister and you. It is good that you two have come together, but while you are mooning about like a buffalo calf,"—a bit of a smile graced his lips— "Many Coups is spreading doubt about you among the lodges. He is strongly questioning your presence among The People and thinks that you should be questioned in open council, maybe even tested in the sun dance."

"What should I do, friend?" asked Bryan. "How can I stop Many Coups?"

"He has made no direct accusation, or you could challenge him directly, and it would be decided in a trial by combat," replied his friend. "You should talk to Faces West about appearing before the council of elders or even the sun dance."

Bryan had seen the scars on the chests of some of the warriors, and in response to his question, he was told of the sun dance ceremony that some warriors performed to validate their worthiness and commitment.

Their skin on both sides of their chest was slashed and rawhide strips run through the slits. These ropes were then hung from a pole, and the sun dancer leaned back to put pressure on the wounds and danced in a circle around the pole, gradually increasing the pressure until finally, the rope pulled through the slits in their skin, releasing them. It usually took hours, and in some extreme rituals, the dancer was hoisted aloft, his feet off the ground, until the flesh parted. There were usually a number of sun dancers, sometimes whole warrior societies of a dozen or more. One sun dance was usually enough for a lifetime, but on occasion, a warrior felt the need to further prove his worth and repeated the ritual.

Bryan had no particular desire to prove himself in this manner, preferring instead to use a more direct means, such as a challenge to Many Coups. He sought out the chief to seek his counsel.

Faces West listened to the young man. He was aware of the whisper campaign being initiated by Many Coups, but other than counseling the young war leader, he could do nothing until Bry-Yan asked him to step into the matter.

"He has not challenged you directly," he said. "But this does not prevent you from challenging him. If you do, though, he has the choice of how to settle the matter. It should be a contest of strength and skill and does not have to involve weapons."

"Can I challenge him to a contest of some sort?" asked Bryan. "Maybe a race or hand-to-hand fight."

"He is too smart to accept a challenge to fight you. He is aware that not any two or even three men could best you. You will have to offer something which Many Coups thinks that he can win," answered Faces West. "Let me think about this for a while. I want to talk to

Many Moons too...see if he has any ideas. We want this talk of his stopped too."

Later, Bryan told Strong Woman of his conversation with the chief. She was familiar with the ways of her people and knew that the chief's counsel was good, but she was also a realist.

"If anything should go wrong and you lose this test, I will go away with you," she stated emphatically. "I have faith in your skills, but Many Coups is a skilled warrior too, and he is very tricky. You will have to be on your guard at all times."

BRYAN'S TEST

After conferring with the old shaman and the chief, Bryan returned to the lodge of White Bull, where his friend was waiting with his sister to hear the strategy laid out by their elders. Bryan related the discussion to them. Neither was surprised by anything they heard.

"It is the way of The People—that only a direct challenge is responded to by direct action," said White Bull. "Many Coups knows this and that if you challenge him, it will be on his terms. He can continue his talk as long as he does nothing that can be considered a challenge to you."

"What would constitute a challenge?" asked Bryan.

"Any personal insult to you or your family. A direct threat against you or even an accusation of cowardice would entitle you to seek satisfaction," replied the Indian. "Many Coups will avoid giving you that chance. He will want to test you on his terms. You could show your courage and worth by the sun dance ritual though and avoid any confrontation with him. He will be forced to stop his talk, or it could then be considered a direct challenge."

Bryan was in a quandary. He knew that he had to stop the talking of Many Coups and would have preferred to confront him, use his martial arts skills to again defeat the brave, and cancel out the questions he had raised. He felt sure that he could beat his enemy in hand-to-hand combat without killing him. In some other contest, he could not be sure a nonfatal solution would be his option. On the other hand, he did not particularly want to undergo the painful ritual of the sun dance, if he could avoid it. He was confident of his ability to withstand the pain through Zen mind control but could not see the sense of the self-inflicted torture for himself though he could understand the warriors' need for such obvious proof of their courage and commitment to their way of life.

He hoped that Faces West or Many Moons could find an answer to his dilemma, so he returned to the lodge of the chief and was bade to enter. After the ritual pleasantries, he inquired of Faces West as to whether he saw any alternatives to those previously outlined. The chief was not able to offer any and indicated that he and the shaman had discussed the matter at length but could not see any way for Bryan to avoid either a confrontation or the sun dance.

Back in her lodge, Strong Woman's fertile mind was at work. She knew that her lover would probably be forced to challenge Many Coups and, thus, fight him on his terms, increasing his chance of coming to harm, or he would seek vindication in the sun dance, neither of which was, to her, the proper alternative. She was confident that her man could defeat Many Coups in weaponless combat but knew that if he challenged the brave, he would be required to fight with weapons, which he was just now becoming familiar with.

Now, she thought, *if only there is a way to get Many Coups to issue the challenge.*

While Strong Woman was trying to come up with a plan to maneuver Many Coups into making the challenge so that Bryan would have the choice of the form the contest would take. Bryan himself was going over the matter with his friend, White Bull. But, no matter how they looked at it, there seemed to be no alternative but for Bryan to issue a direct challenge to Many Coups.

"What do you think that his choice of combat will be?" asked Bryan.

"He is good with all weapons, but he would probably choose spears because with a knife, he would have to close with you and he does not want that," White Bull offered. "It might favor you, though, because he will assume that you will use spear techniques, not knowing that your karate will enable you to use the spear like a Bo, particularly, if we select one with a very heavy shaft."

White Bull continued, "If he does select a knife, he will be at a disadvantage too though he is very fast, and you will have to be wary."

"What about the sun dance?" queried Bryan.

"It would prove that you are a man of courage and worth. If he continued his negative talk, it could be considered a challenge, but it would be for the council to say," said his friend.

"It would seem that the quickest and surest way to approach the matter is to challenge him," stated Bryan emphatically. "And that is how I want it to be—quick. We have other fish to fry." Bryan used an American metaphor, roughly translated into Cheyenne.

White Bull looked at him quizzically. "We have what?"

Bryan grinned. "An old expression. It means we have more important tasks ahead, and I should dispose of this Many Coups thing first. How do I challenge him?"

"You can go to his lodge, stand outside, and loudly insult him. He will have to respond," replied White Bull.

"And then?" Bryan asked.

"He will challenge you to meet him in combat and will name his choice of weapons. You will be expected to accept. The combat will take place as soon as you each have armed yourselves. The elders will be called to witness the contest," responded the Cheyenne. "They will set the rules, depending upon the degree of insult they feel he has suffered. A grievous offense could mean that death is an acceptable outcome. A minor offense could mean a wound cancels it. If you have him at your mercy, you can chose to offer him his life if he withdraws the challenge."

"It is really quite simple," Bryan observed.

THE CHALLENGE

Bryan dressed in his best shirt and breeches. White Bull insisted on painting his face, declaring that he should go to the lodge of Many Coups, dressed for war. He chose to color the top half of Bryan's face bright yellow and the bottom half black. Bryan wished he had a mirror so he could gauge the effect, but the pleased look on his friend's face told him it was dramatic.

He made quite a show of exiting the lodge, with his Bo in hand and the copper knife thrust through his belt. He had a second thought and left the Bo in the weapons rack and strode purposefully through the camp toward Many Coups' lodge. His progress was noted, and soon, there was excited talk, and he strode. People began to appear along the pathway. They were all aware of what was to take place, and there was much excitement. The hubbub grew as he passed through the center of the village and approached his destination.

He stopped in front of the tied open door flap of the lodge. He paused ceremoniously. Out the corner of his eye, he could see that a large crowd had followed him and was waiting expectantly.

Bryan cleared his throat and began to speak, "I am Bry-Yan who has come among The People from a far land. I was treated with the respect offered to those who come in peace, with one exception. He who would wage war on an unarmed stranger was handled as easily as a small child."

There was a tittering from some of the younger members of the crowd, and there were smiles on many of the warriors' faces.

"He who would wage war on me now does it with his tongue since his body failed. I challenge this person to try again with his body, if he is not afraid," he concluded.

There was an excited murmur from the crowd that stilled as Many Coups appeared in the doorway of the lodge. His face looked like a thundercloud, his eyes a slit and mouth twisted in a snarl as he fought for self-control. As he beheld Bryan's paint mask and attire, he spoke, "The pale one has offered a challenge, and I accept. I will test his courage with my lance and shield, and it will be decided who is a child in the ways of battle. Arm yourself, Pale Man, sing your death song because Many Coups will take your scalp this day!"

The warrior stared fiercely at Bryan but was disconcerted to see the pale man grinning at him. Bryan turned on his heel and retraced his steps to White Bull's lodge to retrieve the special, heavy-hafted spear he had fashioned. White Bull fell in beside him, having tailed him to the confrontation.

"Well, my friend, it was well done," he said. "He is angry and will act without thought at first."

Bryan got his spear and shield and began to retrace his path to the center of the village where he knew Many Coups would be waiting. He pushed all negative thoughts from his mind and focused on the task before him. He was confident that when the first move was made, his training and instincts would take over.

White Bull was at his side, and then Strong Woman fell in on his other side.

"Silence this coyote quickly, my man, and return to the lodge for your meal," she said and then turned back toward the lodge.

When he arrived at the village center, most of the tribe was already there. Faces West and the shaman were there with the other tribal elders. Many Coups was standing to one side of this group, having already stated his case.

When Bryan stopped in front of him, Faces West spoke, "You have offered insult and challenge to Many Coups, Bry-Yan, and he has elected to test your word with his lance. The insult is not grievous, but Many Coups has pled that he has lost face and insists that only your death will cleanse this insult. This is his choice and can only be changed by he who has the advantage. You will fight inside the circle we draw on the earth. Any attempt to flee the circle by either combatant will be handled by warriors. Only a winner may leave the circle by his choice."

A circle was drawn in the earth, about fifty feet across. The chief ordered the combatants into it and then stepped out.

Many Coups took a defensive position, shield covering his middle and spear outthrust, and began to circle toward Bryan.

Bryan looked at him with disdain and said loudly, "I do not need a shield against this one who fights best with his mouth." And he tossed his shield behind him. He knew that it would be a hindrance to his Bo fighting techniques but figured to see if he could rile his opponent, maybe make him less cautious.

His must have worked because Many Coups looked as if he would burst a blood vessel as he choked with rage. He moved forward rapidly, jabbing with his lance. Bryan took the shaft of his weapon in both hands, holding it "at the ready" as the Indian closed on him.

Many Coups thrust hard at his midsection, and Bryan parried the lance and, in one continuous motion, stepped past the spear point and swung the other end of the Bo/spear against the Indian's spear-holding arm. The hard blow startled Many Coups, who almost dropped his lance. A low murmur ran through the onlookers. The brave recovered quickly and drew back. Bryan pursued his advantage, rotating the other end of the staff under the other's lance, driving it upward. He swung the other end again, hard against the Indian's ribcage. Many Coups grunted with pain. Thrusting hard with the end, Bryan struck his midsection. Many Coups sat down hard, the wind knocked out of him.

Despite his discomfort, the brave maintained a defensive posture, holding his shield in front of him as he struggled to his feet, gasping for breath. He swung his lance wildly in front of him to keep Bryan from closing again.

Bryan's initial tactics were totally unexpected, but now the Indian was alerted, and his natural vitality was returning fast. Bryan circled him slowly, hoping to encourage an attack for him to counter. Many Coups had recovered sufficiently to begin to circle also. His anger was replaced by caution and pain. He would not attack so foolishly again. Bryan feinted with the spear end and had it parried by the shield. He was able to block the counterthrust and struck hard at the shield again, driving the brave back a step. Bryan dropped down, letting the Bo slide in his hands until he had it by the end while swinging it hard under the brave's defenses. He was rewarded by the stinging shock of contact against Many Coups' shin.

The warrior gasped in pain, and there was a roar from the crowd as he staggered and nearly went down. Stepping in with an overhand sweep, Bryan brought the Bo down hard, aiming at the head of his opponent. Many Coups saw the blow coming and raised his shield. The hard shaft glanced off the shield and struck the brave on the trapezius, where the neck and shoulder meet. Sweeping the Bo around, Bryan struck the warrior's spear hard and saw it leave his hand and fly out to the edge of the circle.

Bryan knew that the fight should be over, but he hadn't counted on the bravery of Many Coups. His face clouded with pain, and he cast aside his shield and drew a knife from his belt. He lunged awkwardly at Bryan who had started to relax his guard. The brave's leg buckled, and his thrust missed Bryan's stomach but grazed his side just below his ribs. Bryan, blood streaming from the cut, stepped forward quickly, stepped on the brave's wrist, twisted the knife from his hand, and held the point against his throat.

"I give you your life. You are too brave a warrior to lose it over a trifle." He rose and walked to the chief while an approving sound rose from the onlookers. He handed the chief the knife, turned, and left the circle for his woman's lodge.

Strong Woman awaited him with open arms and, without a sound, went to work on the shallow cut in his side. She packed the wound with a medicinal plant and covered it with a thin piece of well-tanned leather and bound it in place with a wide belt of the same material.

"It will leave a small reminder of your encounter, but nothing else," she said.

THE PAWNEE GIRL

Talks Fast had been living among the Cheyenne now for about two months, and she had been treated better than she had expected. Her captor, Many Coups, had turned her over to his mother who kept his lodge as he was unmarried. He was usually gone somewhere with his lodge brothers, hunting, raiding, or the like, so she was often alone with the older woman, and because there were so few people in the lodge, there was not enough to occupy two women. As a result, she was able to get most of the work done by herself. Her willingness to work impressed her guardian who treated her kindly.

The maiden liked this clan group. There were a number of young, nice-looking warriors, so her prospects were looking better for a good marriage. Her captor would be a good catch for someone, but Talks Fast thought that he was too vain and haughty for her tastes. The big brave who was a companion of the Pale Man also caught her eye, and she knew that he had been looking at her as well. From what she had been able to learn, he was unmarried, his lodge being kept by his mother and sister, and by the looks of things, the sister would be moving out and building a lodge with the Pale Man.

She was maneuvering for an opportunity to speak with the sister, but her planning was interrupted by her master's challenge and defeat by the Pale Man. He was severely injured with badly bruised ribs and shin and a broken collarbone and required care. Also, he demanded a lot of attention.

At first, during his convalescence, he was quiet and brooding, the anguish of his defeat had humbled him. As he began to heal, he also began to berate both his mother and her when they did not respond fast enough to his needs and demands. Finally, the mother had enough after he had snapped rudely at her.

"I am your mother, not your slave," she said very sharply. "This girl is your slave, but I will not let you continue to treat her poorly just because you feel bad, and you will certainly stop treating your mother badly, or you can cook and care for yourself!"

Many Coups was taken aback. He did not expect this from his mother, who bore him, suckled him, and coddled and fawned on him, her only son. He knew she could make good on her threat because his sister, her warrior husband, and their children lived just down the village street, and their lodge had room for two women who worked well.

Talks Fast had just about given up hope of meeting the big brave, White Bull, when he showed up at their lodge and asked for permission to enter, which grudgingly given by Many Coups. She faded into the background when he entered and was offered a seat. He looked even bigger up close and was very handsome. She felt her stomach quiver as she looked at him.

White Bull got right to the point. "I have come at the request of Bry-Yan. He has asked me to arrange for him to meet with you. He says that The People have too many other tribes as enemies that we should not have enemies in our camp. He seeks an accord with you."

Many Coups was surprised. As the defeated party, he should be the one to seek favor of his victor, particularly since he had been spared an ignoble death with his own knife, but the Pale Man was coming to him. He wondered what his real reason was, but the only way to find out was to agree to a meeting. He assented.

As White Bull rose to leave, his eyes sought out the Pawnee girl. She saw his look and moved to open the door flap for him. As he passed, he looked very intently into her eyes, setting her heart aflutter. *He is definitely interested*, she thought.

She knew she was a comely maiden, smooth skinned and even featured, tall and strongly built with full breasts, small waist, and full hips. She hoped that he was interested in more than just lying with a captive female as she had much more to offer. She was a good cook, tanned and sewed well, and kept a good lodge. Her man would have good clothes, a clean lodge, a full stomach, and warm, willing bedmate.

White Bull was thinking of the Pawnee girl as he strode back to his lodge. She was very attractive, and he could see her interest in him. He would talk to his mother and sister about her. Maybe he could trade for her with Many Coups.

Upon arrival at the tepee, he told Bry-Yan that Many Coups would meet with him later that day. Since it was early afternoon, they would meet just before the evening meal. If Many Coups were a gracious host, it would be a good sign.

BRYAN MAKES PEACE

Many Moons spoke, "Many Coups has too much pride. You defeated him a second time, and his pride will not let him forgive or forget. He is a good hunter and warrior. If age adds humility to his other attributes, he could become a leader of The People. We must do what we can to help heal his spirit."

"I think that you are right," said Faces West. "He has much to offer. It would be a sorrow to lose him to his pride." He looked at Bryan beside him.

Bryan had come to ask to meet with these two elders because he could see that his conflict with the young warrior was an unsettling influence in the tribe. Even though many people thought he was justified and that Many Coups had needed taking down a peg or two, it was still making people choose sides. He learned from the old shaman that rifts like this had occasionally split up a clan group like theirs, and he wanted to end it even if it meant leaving himself.

"Do you think that he would respond to an overture from me?" he queried. "I would seek his favor, if it would stop the dissention."

"It might appeal to his pride," mused the chief.

"It is worth an attempt," added the shaman.

So Bryan sent White Bull to ask for a meeting with the wounded warrior. He knew too that his friend needed little encouragement to make the call because he had been mooning around about the captive Pawnee girl and would appreciate the chance to see her.

White Bull returned with news of Many Coups's agreement to a meeting.

Bryan said, "Was the Pawnee girl there? If so, I am surprised that you had time to talk to Many Coups."

White Bull grinned sheepishly. "Yes, she was there. She is even prettier up close too."

Bryan thought that it was amusing—how this big brave had avoided any entanglements, playing the field some, and now he was smitten by a girl he had seen up close only now. It was, as the Italians of later time said, "the thunderbolt" had hit him.

Later that afternoon, Bryan bathed and dressed with care in the finery made for him by Strong Woman, then headed to the lodge of Many Coups where he was bade enter. The warrior indicated he was to sit across from him, then took his pipe from his case and made a ceremony of filling it with a savory tobacco and herb mixture, tamping and lighting it with a coal brought by his mother.

After puffing smoke at the six sacred directions, he passed the pipe to Bryan, who followed suit. These actions impressed upon Bryan that Many Coups was receptive to an overture, or he would not have honored him with the pipe ceremony. *The brave might be too proud and arrogant, but he is no fool,* he thought.

"I am pleased to see that your injuries are healing well. Your courage and tenacity are very great, and I was forced to extend myself to save injury to me," offered Bryan. The brave grunted a polite assent.

Bryan could immediately see that this was the right tact as suggested by the old Shaman and as some of the tenseness left the Indian.

"I come to you, seeking peace. We may never be friends, but we do not have to be enemies. The People have enemies enough with the Pawnee and Dakota and Kiowa all around us," continued Bryan.

He went on, "My coming among you was as much a surprise to me as it was to The People. The same magic that brought me here may take me back. I have no way of knowing. But you will be here with your people. I wish there to be peace between us while I am with The People."

"It is true what you say, Pale Man. The People have many enemies. We should make peace." Some of Many Coups's pride had healed enough from Bryan's concessions that he was able to be gracious.

"I think that we make a wise decision to put our problems aside," Bryan added.

Many Coups motioned to his mother and the slave girl who had been waiting at the rear of tepee, and the women began to prepare the evening meal.

"Please take the meal with us, Pale Man," said the Brave.

THE QUEST BEGINS

Bryan related the events of his meeting with Many Coups to the old shaman and Faces West later that evening. They were pleased that the problem between the two men appeared to be solved, or at least diminished, by Bryan's actions.

After the chief had left the shaman's lodge, the old man addressed his young protégé. "I think that your time among The People grows short," he stated. "You have prepared our warriors well in the martial arts and strategy, and we are better able to defend our village and hunting grounds because of your visit. I think you should seek the answers to your questions about your presence in this land since I think it is the result of more than just an old shaman's magical call. I think that you should travel to the land of the Pawnee and find this other pale man the captive girl has told about. To make your way among them, you should take her and your friend, White Bull, who speaks their language."

"I do not want to think of leaving The People though I know that I must. I have grown comfortable here, made friends, and have learned much. I will leave a richer person, one who hopes to return," Bryan said.

"You will seek and find your destiny, my young friend. The spirits will be with you. Listen to them when they visit you," the old man went on.

Bryan rose and returned to White Bull's lodge, already feeling the loss of the old man's counsel and friendship. He had found a place here among the people, one so well suited to him that he had almost forgotten about his former life and the possibility of returning.

Bryan and Strong Woman had been meeting secretively along the wooded creek bank and other private places, making love and exploring each other's bodies and minds. Bryan did not want this relationship to end nor his friendship with White Bull, but it had entered his thoughts that whatever had brought him to this land could also whisk him away just as easily. He knew that it was time to seek some answers.

He told Strong Woman and White Bull of the shaman's advice. Strong Woman was the first to respond.

"I will go with you too, Bry-Yan. I intend to be with you wherever you go to seek your destiny... You see, you are my destiny!"

White Bull was affirmative also.

"We will travel together, my brother, to the Pawnee and beyond."

Bryan said with a grin, "It would not be because the Pawnee girl goes with me, would it?"

"It could have some influence on my decision, but I would go with you anyway" was the smiling response.

They spent the remainder of the evening and into the night planning what they would need for the journey.

In the morning, Bryan went to the lodge of Many Coups and told him of the shaman's suggestion that the Pawnee captive should go with them to her people. The brave was inwardly so pleased to see his nemesis departing that he agreed readily to give him the captive girl. He called her into the lodge and told her to gather her possessions and go with the Pale Man as she now belonged to him.

With the girl in tow, he returned to White Bull's lodge where Strong Woman and her mother greeted her in a pleasant manner. White Bull appeared pleased.

Bryan learned that White Bull's mother would be moving in with her daughter's family when her son and daughter departed with Bryan and the Pawnee maiden. Any possession they could not take would be divided up among relatives, to be returned or replaced when they returned.

They quizzed the girl as to the location of the clan where there was another pale man, but since she did not know precisely, it was decided to start their search at the girl's village.

Bryan called together his training group and informed them of the decision to go west. A number of the young men wanted to accompany them, but Bryan told them that his vision had not indicated he should have a large party with him on his quest. Bryan arranged that several of the most advanced students should continue to lead the classes, expanding them to include all the warriors, and even any women and children who wanted to learn martial arts. He stressed the importance of basic techniques and kata as the learning emphasis and strongly encouraged the involvement of the women and children.

Back at the lodge, he gathered together his weapons, tools, and clothing to make up a pack he would carry west. He made sure to include several pairs of moccasins and a quantity of soap.

The others had already prepared their packs. All was set for their departure before first light on the morrow.

JOURNEY HOME
FOR THE PAWNEE GIRL

The early morning chill penetrated his shirt and leggings when he stepped from the lodge. By his calculations, Bryan figured that he had arrived in the land of The People in mid Spring, probably April, and now, nearly five months later, fall was fast approaching in the south-central plains. They would soon need warmer clothing for their travels but would have to trade for it or hunt for hides from which to make it as their limited packs could not possibly hold all that they would need—heavy robes, coats, fur hats, and mittens.

The other three travelers exited the lodge and helped each other hoist their packs and settle them on their backs, the straps over their shoulders. With White Bull in the van, they left the village by the main trail west, moving at a fast walk in the very dim light, two hours before the dawn.

By the time the sun had begun to peek over the horizon at their backs, they had traveled about seven or eight miles. They paused for a drink and a chew of jerky. It was their plan to travel at a brisk pace during the daylight hours, eating a midday meal on the run, their main meal coming at nightfall, when they made camp. On the first night, maybe two, they would have a fire, but as they moved closer to the Pawnee village home of Talks Fast, they would make a dark camp to avoid detection. They wanted to enter the camp during daylight with the Pawnee girl to lead the way so as to avoid a hostile confrontation. Once in the camp, Plains Indian courtesy would prevail, and they would be safe until they left.

There was little conversation as they traveled, all of them being alert to their surroundings as they walked, but Bryan noticed that White Bull was keeping close to the Pawnee girl. It was quite apparent that they both felt the same attraction to the other. As one who was also smitten, it pleased Bryan to see the same thing happening to his friend.

It was also apparent to him that the women did not receive nor did they expect any special consideration or help. The packs they carried were as big and heavy as the one he bore, and they both seemed to be carrying them as easily, or maybe even easier, than he. He had noticed that though the Cheyenne were solicitous of their women and respected them, the men did little to assist them in their duties, regardless of how heavy the task, nor did the women want their help. With few exceptions, they readily accepted the role tradition assigned to them. These exceptions were notable in that there had always been, and were now, women who were warriors and hunters, seemingly as suited to this role as any of the men. By the same token, men who had no affinity for these pursuits were allowed to assume any role they felt comfortable in, totally accepted by their peers, with no discrimination nor harassment.

At dusk, they were still in familiar territory, well within the normal hunting range of the village of The People. They found shelter in a copse of trees through which a brook rambled. The women sought a supply of firewood as White Bull made a fire with the small fire drill he carried. A pemmican stew was made in a small vessel and they talked as they dined.

"What reception will we get from your people, Talks Fast?" asked White Bull, partly in sign, part in Pawnee.

"They will be happy to see me, I am sure, and you will be well received for returning me to them," she answered. "They will listen to your story of the pale one's vision quest and honor it."

"Will they know where we can find the other pale man?" White Bull asked.

"He is told to be among the Skidi, Wolf People, who are far to the west, near the mountains which reach to the sky," she said. "There will be those among my people who can tell you where there main camp is located."

Unlike the Cheyenne, who lived in tepees year around, the Pawnee only used these portable shelters while on hunting trips, preferring to establish more permanent villages of rounded, earthen lodges. When they knew the location of the Skidi village, it would be easily found. The Pawnee still practiced agriculture, raising maize, beans, and squash, but they, like the Cheyenne, were dependent on the buffalo for most of their necessities. The Cheyenne referred to their life after their migration from near the Great Lakes as "when they lost the corn," indicating that they too had once been farmers as well as hunters. Much of this Bryan had learned from the tales of the old shaman, Many Moons.

Bryan and Strong Woman settled into a leafy nest, covered by a light robe that they shared. In the dim light of the fading coals, he could see that White Bull and the girl were settling down near each other, and he smiled inwardly as he felt Strong Woman snuggling against his back, and he was filled with contentment.

They were up and ready to move on well before the next dawn. This close to home, they were not particular about removing signs of their camp, so as soon as they had gathered themselves, they headed out at a brisk pace.

Shortly after the dawn, they were passing through an area of low, shrub-like growth when they flushed a covey of prairie chicken. Bryan and White Bull each brought down a bird with their throwing sticks. The brave had noted where several others had landed, and while Bryan retrieved the two, he went after the others and succeeded in knocking one down. The birds were hung together with a thong and slung across White Bull's pack for cleaning at the stream nearby. These birds would be cooked tonight over what would be their last fire until they reached the Pawnee village. After that, it would be jerky.

That night, Bryan estimated that they had covered close to one hundred miles in two hard days of travel.

The birds were spitted, cooked, and wolfed down, and they all fell into their sleeping robes. Bryan noted that White Bull and Talks Fast made no pretense and snuggled in together.

In late afternoon on the third day, they saw signs of other travelers. In a sandy creek bottom, they found several tracks. They were too obscure to make out details other than men made them. Sometimes tribal identification could be made by moccasin patterns, but it was not the case this time. It was a good assumption that they were made by hostiles this far from the Cheyenne village, so they proceeded with caution. That night was a dark camp on a brushy slope well above a small creek. Since animals and man all sought water, they avoided surprise detection by bedding down away from the stream. They chewed a little jerky and rolled into their robes.

Sleep did not come at first to Bryan. He lay there with his woman in his arms and thought about his life, before and now. He had always been searching before, looking for a satisfying career, seeking activities that challenged his physical side. All his friends were similarly involved, but there had always been something missing. It had been play; their survival had not depended upon their skills. Now, he was in a world where what he was very good at counted the most. He was truly in his element. He ached some for his family and friends, but in his mind, he was not sure he would want to return if he could discover how. This woman in his arms had come to mean more to him than anyone or anything ever had before, but he still felt a sense of loyalty to his parents and knew that they would be very concerned over his absence. He fell asleep, wondering what his father would say to him about the situation.

The next day, shortly after midday, they came across signs of a successful buffalo hunt. A shallow but steep ravine bore all the signs of twenty or more of the great beasts having been butchered there. The drag marks of heavily laden, dog-drawn travois pointed away to the northwest, so they headed that way. The sign was at least a day or more old, so there was little likelihood they would overtake the hunters, even at their quickened pace.

It was dusk when they topped a rise and saw a slight glow in the sky about a mile distant. It was the cooking fires of the Pawnee camp. Bryan could almost smell and taste the buffalo meat cooking. They drew closer to the camp and concealed themselves in a copse of trees on the far side of a ridge away from the camp. In the morning, they would enter the camp as people were rising, and Talks Fast would take them to the lodge of her parents.

THE SURPRISE

Bryan was awakened suddenly by a hand over his mouth and struggled a moment before he realized it was White Bull whispering in his ear to be still.

"Quiet. Listen. There are some people moving along the slope below us," came White Bull's hushed voice in his ear.

Bryan could hear slight sounds of passage, but his untrained ear could not discern what or how many it was.

"At least ten, maybe more...and they are moving quietly, too quietly to be from the Pawnee camp," came the whisper again. "It is probably a raiding party coming to attack."

The moon was not out, but there was enough starlight for Bryan to see that the women were awake and waiting quietly for the danger to pass. After fifteen minutes or so, White Bull moved from his side and faded into the darkness. After another twenty or thirty minutes, he reappeared.

"It is a party of Omaha, at least fifteen of them, painted for war. With this many of them and the village so small, they probably will attack rather than sneak into the village to steal a few things," he said.

"What shall we do?" inquired Bryan. "We should help the Pawnee since we are looking for their favor."

"We will circle the camp in the other direction and enter from the opposite side from the Omaha hiding place. If we can warn the people, it will be the Omaha who are surprised, not the Pawnee," responded White Bull.

The women agreed that this was the best course, so they circled the camp and snuck stealthily along until Talks Fast was able to point out her parents' lodge. While the three of them waited, she crept in. There was a brief flurry of noise that quickly subsided, and then, her figure appeared in the entrance and motioned them in.

When the door flap had closed, a fire in the center of the lodge was stirred into life, illuminating the interior. Unlike the skin tepee, this light would not be visible from the outside.

Bryan took in the scene of Talks Fast's family dwelling. Her father was a large, hawk-nosed warrior with the roached scalp lock preferred by his people, the sides of his head shorn of hair. He was responding without question to his daughter's return and the alarm she brought. He was looking over the companions she had brought, his eyes widening at the sight of Bryan, whose pale skin and his size was an oddity. Her mother, who had stirred up the fire, was slipping into a dress while two younger children were still in their sleeping robes but awake and taking in the activity.

After a hurried conversation, the man and his wife left the lodge, being careful not to show too much light.

"They are going to warn the others," said White Bull, who had understood the conversation.

"How will they attack?" asked Bryan.

"They will come out of the sun at first light," replied White Bull. "They are a large-enough party that with surprise, they could take a small village like this, slaughter or drive off the men, and take the women and children as slaves and also to carry their booty."

"We could empty the lodges closest to the anticipated attack point, drawing them further into the village. Warriors could hide in the lodges on either side of the attack route so that when the Omaha passed, these men could attack them from the sides and rear. We would have them surrounded," Bryan strategized aloud. "How many warriors are in this village?" he continued, addressing Talks Fast. White Bull posed the question in Pawnee though she understood some Cheyenne.

"About four hands full," was the response.

"With us two and surprise, that should do it," said Bryan.

When Talks Fast's father returned, his daughter bade him listen to the plan of the Pale Man. White Bull explained what Bryan had in mind, and the man smiled and nodded. He left again to pass among the lodges and lay out the surprise planned for the Omaha.

Just before first light, it was all arranged. The lodges in the direct path of the attack had been vacated, all the warriors dispersed to the lodges along either side of the anticipated attack. All the other warriors were spread among the lodges in the center of the village, in the direct line of attack. What was left was almost like the trap the hunters used for buffalo. A wide, unoccupied opening, warriors along the sides, but instead of a ravine to rush over, there were waiting warriors. Bryan thought later that he couldn't have scripted it better.

Just as if he had written their plan for them, at first light, the attack came out of the east. The painted Omaha warriors swept into the camp, whooping. The warriors who entered the first lodges came out surprised by their vacancy but were swept back into the stream of their companions heading into the center of the village. Just when they thought they had no resistance, Pawnee, dressed for war, appeared from the center lodges. The surprised Omaha drew up but then pressed on, whooping anew, committed to their attack. Then out came other Pawnee, streaming from the surrounding lodges and those that they had passed, and they all fell on the stunned Omaha.

Bryan had joined the attack with his bo/lance and found himself confronting a black-faced, scalp-locked Omaha who was brandishing a stone war club. Bryan feinted with the spear point, and when the Omaha moved to parry with his club, he reversed the thrust and swung the haft hard against the brave's side, felling him. As the man struggled to rise, Bryan brought the Bo down hard on his head, finishing him. He immediately turned to engage another enemy but found that all the attackers had been vanquished. The majority of whom had been wounded or disarmed, but a few still bodies lay on the ground. Not a single Pawnee suffered any more than minor wounds.

There was much whooping and yelling as Pawnee warriors moved on the fallen Omaha and scalped them quickly. Bryan's conquest was just knocked out, so he stood over the fallen brave, so no one would attempt to scalp him.

White Bull appeared at his side. His war paint had begun to run from sweat, and there was a large grin on his face.

"You are a great war leader, Bry-Yan," he said. "Never have I seen so great a victory. Not a single one escaped."

"What will be done to the prisoners?" asked Bryan. "Will they be slaves?"

"Some, but most will go to the fire," responded White Bull. "These Pawnee like to burn their captives to see how brave they are."

Bryan was repulsed. He still had trouble adjusting to the basic cruelty of life on the plains. Hard life created hard people, and the code of bravery said that if your enemies were brave, so were you. If they died well, it honored you, their enemy.

"Take me to the Pawnee chief," said Bryan. "I know something that will better serve him than to burn these men."

In front of the chief, Bryan was surprised to see it was the father of Talks Fast. With White Bull interpreting, Bryan laid out his plan.

"Chief," he began, "who will ever know what befell these Omaha who were foolish enough to attack the Pawnee? Only their absence in their lodges will be noted and soon forgotten. But if you strip these men of their weapons, clothing, bind their hands to poles across their shoulders, and send them back to their village, you will have many voices counseling against attacking the Pawnee again. Their return journey will be worse than your fire and those who make it will be a reminder of what happens to those foolish enough to come painted for war against the Pawnee!"

Bryan could see that the chief was digesting these thoughts. He was nodding as if to himself as he replied.

"The Pale Man gives good counsel. Other than the leader of this war party, we will send them back as you suggest. The leader will go to the fire to please our gods."

He continued, "The Pale Man has shown himself to be a brother of the Cahaui Pawnee, he will always be welcome in our lodges. You will be my guest while you are amongst us."

THE BETROTHAL
OF WHITE BULL

The remaining Omaha, except for the leader of the war party, were stripped, their arms bound to poles across their shoulders, taken to the edge of the village and released, otherwise unharmed. Their return trip, probably at least a week or ten days long, would be hard, and they would think twice about raiding the Pawnee again.

In the chief's lodge, the women prepared a sumptuous meal of buffalo, corn cakes baked on hot stones, and a gruel of corn, beans, and squash, which Bryan recognized as succotash.

The chief, Spotted Calf, leaned against his backrest, Bryan and White Bull on his right, the place of honor, and several of the tribal elders on his left. Spotted Calf brought out his pipe and filled it with an aromatic mixture of wild tobacco and herbs. After each man had puffed smoke to the six sacred directions, the Chief began.

"It is not usual for the Pawnee and Cheyenne to be allied." He signed while speaking softly, making the vee sign for Pawnee and chopping at his index finger for Cheyenne. "We often raid each other, sometimes making war. It has been good for us today, working together against a common foe. I am overjoyed at the return of my daughter, although,"—he looked pointedly at White Bull—"I do not think that she will stay in her father's lodge for long."

The Cheyenne lowered his eyes slightly but acknowledged, with a nod, the truth of this matter.

Spotted Calf went on, "You have saved many lives this day with your actions. The Chaui cannot ever forget this. You are always welcome in peace in our lodges." He then gave each of them a string of shell beads. "Wear this as a token of our brotherhood. All the Pawnee will recognize the sign of Spotted Calf and will honor it."

Bryan spoke and signed a response, White Bull verbalized, "We thank our friends, the Pawnee, for their hospitality and gifts. We are traveling to seek out another pale man who is living with the Skidi people, the Wolf clan of the Pawnee. It is my hope to find another of my people. We ask you to give us directions to find this camp."

"The man you seek is far toward the setting sun, many days travel from here. It is reported that he came among the Skidi a double handful of moons ago. He is a man of magic, a shaman," replied Spotted Calf.

The women began to pass around clay bowls of succotash and sizzling meat on skewers. The Pawnee, with their permanent villages, had developed some of the potters craft and had bowls and other fired clay dishes.

Nomads like the Cheyenne could not store or transport fragile items like this.

As they ate, the discussion continued, interrupted occasionally by a polite belch. The food was very good, and Bryan welcomed the taste of the vegetables and corn bread.

White Bull said, "The vision of my brother, Bry-Yan, is to seek his destiny in the west. He thinks that your Skidi brothers' pale man is of his people, so he wants to speak with him. My brother too is a wizard, a master of fighting arts. He has been teaching the warriors of The People to fight as he does, with hands and feet and staffs of wood. With no weapons, he twice vanquished our greatest fighter, who was fully armed."

The Pawnee looked at Bryan with new interest.

"How did he come to be among the Cheyenne?" inquired Spotted Calf.

"He came, like your Skidi pale one, a handful of moons ago. He knows not how he came to be in the land of the People, it being some magic he does not understand," answered White Bull.

"He looks to be as strong as a buffalo bull," commented one of the elders.

"He is and is a great warrior," came the reply.

Spotted Calf said, "I will send someone with you to guide your party to the Skidi village." He gave a humorous sidelong glance at White Bull. "Maybe Talks A Lot should be the one."

Bryan had observed that these Native Americans all had a good sense of humor and liked to tease one another.

White Bull responded, "Spotted Calf, I am a person accompanying my brother on a quest, and I have no right to ask, but I seek your approval... I wish to take Talks Fast as a bride. I do not have the marriage price now, but if you will grant this, I will pay you this dowry when the quest is concluded."

Spotted Calf smiled. "I do not think that I have any choice in the matter. The girl and her mother have decided. She is very valuable, but I place on you the determination of her worth to be paid when your quest is done."

"If all of the hunting grounds were mine, I would pay it!" uttered White Bull emphatically.

"Do not speak too hastily, young man. I may expect you to pay that much," replied Spotted Calf with a big grin. "However, I thought that she was lost to us, and you returned her from your people, so her price is peace between us, you and me. Whatever else you decide to include will be cheerfully accepted."

He summoned his daughter, and when she arrived, he advised her that White Bull had offered a great marriage price for her and asked her what she was thinking. Her quick response was for her father to accept. With this, White Bull and Talks Fast were betrothed.

THE SKIDI PAWNEE

White Bull had obviously been scheming.

"You realize," he said to Bryan, "that if you want a marriage with my sister, I, as the senior male in her family, will set the bridal price. I think that whatever it is, it will be at least equal to my cost for Talks Fast."

"In my land," lied Bryan with a laugh, "the prospective bride's parents pay for the groom. The men in my land are very valuable."

"I am sure that you are the exception," said White Bull. "Maybe your father will accept some worn-out moccasins or a broken bow."

"Enough," said Strong Woman, threatening them both with the back of her hand. "You two should be preparing for the journey to the Skidi, not teasing each other. If we had to pay for husbands, we would both certainly opt for better prospects than you two."

The men returned to packing their traveling necessities.

The next morning, before dawn, the four travelers departed from the Chaui Pawnee village of Spotted Calf, traveling west-northwest at a fast pace.

The terrain had been gradually rising, almost unnoticeably, until Bryan figured that they must be several thousand feet above sea level. Looking back, he could see the land falling away to the east. He surmised that if this land was the same as in his time, they would be somewhere in central Colorado. The land was quite arid, though not really desert, and there was a lot of low scrub growth among the calf-high buffalo grass.

On the third day, they could see clouds on the horizon that did not seem to get any closer as they traveled. Late in the day, Bryan realized that he was seeing the "mountains which reach to the sky" and their snowcapped peaks, not clouds.

Late in the day, they encountered a hunting party of Pawnee. While the other three remained behind, Talks Fast approached them, identified her party and their quest. She turned and motioned the others to join her.

"They have heard already of the great victory over the Omaha and our pale man who helped the Pawnee," She told the others. "They welcome us to accompany them to their village, which is where their pale visitor lives."

It was nearly dusk when they arrived in the Skidi village. It was comprised of large, earth-covered lodges, much like the Chaui camp. The outskirts contained fields of maize, melons, and beans that looked well tended, with long raised rows of plants. Bryan realized later that they used some form of irrigation.

One of the hunters had run ahead of the party, so there was a reception party awaiting their arrival, the clan chief, shaman, and elders, who conducted Bryan's group to a large lodge in the center of the village.

When they entered, Bryan saw immediately another white man rising from his seat to greet them. He smiled and offered his hand.

"Hello, I'm Charles Branson," he said in English. "When the runner brought word or another white man in the Chaui village, I couldn't believe it. You speak English, I hope."

Bryan took his hand. "Yes, I do. I'm Bryan McKay. How long have you been here? How did you get here? What do you..."

"Wait a minute, Bryan, I can only deal with one thing at a time," came the laughing response. "I don't think that I have any better idea than you do. I just found myself naked in this world... It happened about ten or twelve months ago, by my calculations." Branson continued, "I remember losing control of my car in a rainstorm and sliding into a ditch. That's the last I recall before finding myself here."

"That's pretty much what happened to me," said Bryan. "I went to sleep in a dentist chair and woke up here."

"I'm forgetting my manners," said Branson. "Please, you and your companions, be seated."

Bryan spoke to the other in Cheyenne. "He is from my world, but he knows no more than I do about how we got here. He invites us to be seated in his lodge. We will talk more."

After all were seated, an older Pawnee woman materialized and began to prepare a meal. Soon, the smells of cooking food filled the lodge.

"Tell me about yourself and your experiences here, please, Bryan," said the older man.

Bryan recounted a little of his background and of his five months with The People. When he paused, Branson interjected, "It sounds like you have found a home, son. You seem to have fit right in with these people."

He continued, "I calculate that we are in a time somewhere in the mid-fourteenth or early fifteenth century. These people are well developed socially but still in the tag end of the Stone Age, much like they were when the Spaniards first came to the New World."

"Yeah, I did notice the absence of horses, which came with the Spanish conquistadors," added Bryan. "But what about the fields around the village. I didn't know that the Plains Indians had any agriculture."

Branson offered, "Most Native Americans had some degree of agronomy. Less on the plains than in the Southwest and some other areas, but I have been helping some, that's my background. I taught range science at Texas A & M. I have shown them how to better irrigate their crops, and it seems to be working. We've had a bumper crop this year."

"Were you in Texas when you...you know, came here?" asked Bryan.

"Yes... Why, where were you?"

"In my hometown, Jasper, Pennsylvania."

"This is all so puzzling," said the older man. "There doesn't seem to be any connection with geographics and our being here. I just can't figure it."

At this point, the meal was served, again in clay bowls.

"My first priority has been to survive and adapt," said Bryan during a pause in the eating. "We can work out the 'whys' later, if we are ever able to work them out."

"Let's get you folks settled in. We'll talk more later on," said Charles Branson.

THE PROFESSOR

As they ate, the older man filled them in on his background and time with the Skidi Pawnee. Charles Branson was forty-eight years old, though he appeared younger, and a full professor at Texas Agricultural and Mechanical University, home of the famous Texas Aggies, one of the finest schools in the country for engineers and agronomists. His specialty was range science, which involved the management of cattle ranches as well as the food the cattle were fed. As such, he had the knowledge to improve vastly the agriculture of the Skidi people through irrigation, crop rotation, and other means, and he had done so in his five months on the plains.

The Professor proclaimed that he was of American Indian ancestry, Comanche mixed with Scottish and that he was a widower with no children though he proudly pointed out that his Pawnee bride was carrying his child. In his time with the Skidi, he had introduced them to irrigation, running water from the nearby stream through canals to the fields of maize, squash, and beans, which now formed a greater portion of the dict of the Skidi.

Some of their harvest, they ate fresh, but most of it was dried for later use. He was examining the possibility of adding other crops to their farming, onions and herbs, which he readily identified as growing wild in the area. He said he would like to find some chilies, as he loved spicy food, and it was a good blood cleanser as well.

Though he was not a survivalist like Bryan, he had adapted well, fitting into the life on the Great Plains with enthusiasm. He had married a middle-aged woman of thirty-five years, a widow, and was now going to have a family.

After the meal, he and Bryan continued their talk. He brought forth a pipe and tamped in some tobacco, commenting, "I didn't see any warning label on the plants, so I guess it's okay to smoke this stuff."

Bryan, never a smoker, did enjoy a few puffs after the meal with the professor as did White Bull. Bryan had been translating some as they went, so the others were following the gist of the conversation.

The professor, as Bryan had begun to think of him, was curious as to how they both had come to be here but had no idea how to start to find out no more than Bryan had. Like Bryan, he was not sure that he would return to his time and land if he could find the means. He felt more productive than he ever had before.

"Maybe we are here as guides or trail markers to an alternative future…a better one than that that awaits them in our world."

After their smoke, the professor said, "How about an after-dinner brandy?"

Bryan was surprised. "Sure. Did you import some from France?"

"No," said the professor. "But I have a reasonable facsimile." He produced a gourd jug with a stopper and several smaller gourd drinking vessels. Pouring a healthy tot into three of them, he offered two to Bryan and White Bull.

"Corn cider," he explained. "I have no copper tubing for a still, so I settled for a straight fermentation. It has a little kick but is pleasant after a hard day at the office," he continued, grinning.

Bryan took a sip. It was surprisingly smooth and went down easily. He could see White Bull smacking his lips appreciatively as he downed his drink.

"That's good!" exclaimed Bryan. "How much of this did you make?"

"Well, I didn't have to worry about the alcohol tax and firearms, boys, so I made about twenty-five gallons, which I fermented in the big gourds using much the same method as our early colonials did with apple cider. I made a 'trap' of reeds so the gas could escape, but no air could enter. It seems to have worked."

The men enjoyed another "brandy" while they discussed what their next move was.

"Stay with us here a while," offered Branson. "Maybe, between the two of us, we can figure out some answers. I have had the Skidi inquiring as to whether any other pale men have been seen elsewhere, but no word has come back. Maybe we are the only ones who got transported or whatever happened." He went on, "I suspect, however, that we are just a few of those who have traveled the Spirit World."

Bryan relayed the invitation to his companions who agreed. White Bull was somewhat enthusiastic as he could now properly woo and wed Talks Fast. Strong Woman was happy to be with Bryan and not on the move.

The next day, the professor was showing Bryan and White Bull around the camp, particularly the irrigation system in the fields. He had built a small dam, partially diverting the stream into a series of channels that fed the fields. The semi-arid soil had responded by producing the best crop the Skidi had ever known. Plans were being made to expand the fields since they no longer had to depend on the scarce rain.

"One thing that I did bring a stop to was the sacrifice of a girl captive to the Corn God every spring," said the Professor. "I showed the Skidi that they did not have to do that to have a good crop. It was a barbaric custom, which has gone on for centuries, but no more...at least among the Skidi. I am going to visit other villages and teach them our methods... Maybe I can get the practice stopped everywhere among the Pawnee."

Later, Bryan and the professor talked about their plans.

"We seem to both be teaching these primitive people what we know, me the martial arts and you how to farm. Your teachings seem a lot more productive than mine."

"What we both have to teach is important. Without the means to defend themselves, farmers are at the mercy of the nomads. It has been this way ever since man planted the first seed or domesticated the first goat or cow," replied the professor. "Farming and husbandry gave man the ability to settle in one place and develop a science, the arts, and civilization, but he had to be a warrior too to protect his interests."

He continued, "Maybe there is a grand design to our presence here. Maybe we are intended to bring our knowledge, to move these people another rung up the ladder." The Professor went on, "It could be that this is how advances have been made throughout history. There have certainly been some quantum leaps at times in our history, which have never been satisfactorily explained."

"It has occurred to me," said Bryan, "that we may not even be on our world. Instead of traveling in time, maybe we simply were moved another dimension to a parallel world or something like that."

"We may never know," offered the professor. "What we must do is to make the best of the situation and utilize our skills to improve our lot and that of these fine people, each in our own way." He continued, "I don't have any family or close friends that I have left behind, but you have a lot of unfinished business back in Pennsylvania. Maybe you will have a chance to do that. I feel sure that time is moving there as it is here, but I'm not sure how it will work if we pop back and forth between the worlds."

WHITE BULL'S CHALLENGE

Strong Bear did not like the Cheyenne interloper who had the eye of Talks Fast. He had long had his eye on the comely maiden, the daughter of a neighboring chief, Spotted Calf, but she had never given him any sign that she was interested, but in the Pawnee way, that was not always necessary if a warrior had a good marriage price to pay, and Strong Bear had many possessions—buffalo robes, coyote and fox pelts, many flint points for arrows and spears, several fine shields, as well as a lodge in which to house a bride. He was a good hunter and honored warrior. Though not very tall, he had an imposing physique and was often the winner in wrestling matches. The spirits had blessed him with many physical attributes, except for beauty... Strong Bear was very homely. His hair grew down on his brow, giving him a feral appearance, his nose was bulbous and prominent, and youthful skin disease had left his cheeks pockmarked and scarred. This ugliness, which had driven him to succeed as a warrior, also prevented any comely girls from wanting to share his lodge.

Now, the young woman he had desired the most had returned from captivity with a hated Cheyenne brave panting after her. Strong Bear was incensed. He grumbled to the members of his warrior society about the cursed Cheyenne among them until one of the other, tired of the grousing, suggested that if he felt that way, why did he not do something about the Cheyenne...like maybe find an excuse to challenge him!

The suggestion was made as a joke to quiet the grumbling, but it struck a responsive chord. Strong Bear began to think about how he could offer a challenge without violating the chief's hospitality to the Cheyenne party. He began to think that if he defeated the brave, White Bull, he would be elevated in the eyes of the girl, Talks Fast...maybe enough to get her interested in being his bride. Strong Bear's thinking was as twisted as his face; his only desire was to impress the girl.

While Strong Bear plotted, the object of his smoldering hatred was training with his best friend, Bry-Yan. They had resumed their morning workouts as soon as they reached the Skidi village. White Bull had advanced well past the intermediate stage of training and was now being taught advanced forms and techniques. His defensive tactics were progressing to the point that Bry-Yan had to extend himself to penetrate them. He was still a long ways from scoring much on his sensei, but he was confident that he would be able to handle almost anything that came at him. Without any protective gear, their sparring was limited to light to moderate contact only, but White Bull knew that one had only to extend the technique to score a telling blow or kick.

Strong Bear's plotting was going nowhere until he remembered the harvest celebration that would take place a few days hence. The tribe feted the gathering of their crops, and since this year it looked like a bumper crop would be reaped, the festival would be a big event, with feasting and dancing. The men and boys would compete in foot races, archery, spear throwing, and wrestling. It was this last event that was of particular interest to Strong Bear. He would challenge the Cheyenne to a match, defeat him, and claim the girl. He could see it all in his mind.

The whole village was abuzz with preparations for the harvest festival. The braves spent a lot of time practicing for the sporting events they planned on competing in, while the women prepared the feast from the harvest of their plantings, and the meats the men had brought back from hunting forays—buffalo, of course, and the large antlered elk, mule deer, antelope, bear, and a wide variety of small game and fish from the rivers and streams nearby.

Bryan and White Bull planned on giving a martial arts demonstration, both weaponless and with the Bo. They practiced almost from dawn to dark in the week preceding the big event, perfecting their techniques and choreographing their moves together until they were almost flawless, the bo moving with such speed they were almost a blur.

The athletic events would begin at early morning, just after daybreak, starting with the footraces of various distances and then moving to the martial skills of spear throwing for distance and accuracy and then the archery. The final events, just before the start of the big feast, would be the wrestling.

Unlike modern-day collegiate or Greco-Roman wrestling, the Indian form had few rules. Any means could be used to put an opponent on his back since this was basically a fighting technique used against enemies and intended to disarm and disable an opponent. The match ended when one competitor called for quarter or was rendered unconscious or unable to continue due to injury. Serious injury was often the result of these "friendly" matches.

Both Bryan and White Bull planned on competing in the footraces, White Bull in the sprints and Bryan in middle distances. They both arose early on the morning of the event. They warmed up with stretches and a little techniques practice—punching and kicking from the horse stance. They were sweating lightly when the call came for the first race. Bryan accompanied White Bull to the starting line. He was sure that the Cheyenne would be competitive having run against him in the previous months.

The sprint course was a relatively flat area near the river. The braves lined up on a mark made in the earth between two upright poles. The distance was several hundred yards and finished between two more upright poles. Several judges were at the finish line in case there was a close finish as was often the case.

Bryan was surprised at the sizes and shapes of the braves competing in the sprints. Where White Bull was tall, with a barrel chest and long, slender, muscular legs, there were others who didn't look like sprinters, one in particular was largely muscled in his upper body but with crooked, bandy legs. He was exceedingly ugly, with a low brow and bulbous features. He was spending an inordinate amount of time glaring at White Bull when the latter wasn't looking.

At the shout for the start, everyone was off, with White Bull and the ugly one in nearly a dead heat for second place, behind a slender, wiry-looking young man. Gradually, White Bull began to pull ahead and overtake the leader, but the bandy-legged one was still in contention, also overtaking the original leader. As they neared the finish line, the ugly one put on a burst of speed and overtook White Bull, but as he attempted to pass, the Cheyenne found some hidden reserves and held him off, crossing the finish line just a few ticks ahead of the other.

After several sprint heats, a final race was held amongst the winners in all the earlier races. Again, White Bull was pitted against the ugly warrior named Strong Bear, they had learned, who had won another sprint after his second place finish in the first race against the Cheyenne. Again, White Bull prevailed, this time by a larger margin.

Bryan did well in the middle distances, coming in second in his first attempt, and third in another heat. He was pleased with his performance, being more of a long distance runner than middle distance or sprinting.

170

When it came time for the wrestling, neither Bryan nor White Bull had planned on competing but would be spectators instead. Their karate demo would be after all the other events as entertainment for the feasters. Thus they were surprised when the ugly Pawnee, Strong Bear, issued a challenge to White Bull to wrestle. The Indians place great value in "face," so it would be nearly impossible for the Cheyenne to refuse the challenge gracefully.

When they paired off in the center of the circle of rocks, the designated ring for the matches, their differences where quite apparent: Where White Bull was taller than average, the Pawnee was shorter. White Bull was slender of limb, though well muscled and had broad shoulders and a large ribcage. Strong Bear was largely muscled in his chest, shoulders, and arms. His legs were muscled, though somewhat bowed adding to his shortness. Bryan guessed that their body weights were close.

With the signal to begin, the combatants began to circle each other, watching the other for any signs of weakness. Suddenly, Strong Bear rushed in with arms outstretched to grapple with White Bull. The Cheyenne reacted quickly with a stepping sidekick to the chest of the Pawnee, which stopped him in his tracks. Instead of following up with an attack of his own, White Bull delayed, allowing the Pawnee to recover from the surprise. Wary now, Strong Bear circled cautiously around the Cheyenne. Bryan was pleased to see that his friend remembered that "any attack exposes a window of vulnerability," and he awaited the next move by the squat warrior.

After circling some more, a few grunts of dissatisfaction came from the audience. White Bull ignored the noise, but it incensed his opponent who made another move to attack. This time the Cheyenne stepped forward, inside the encircling arms and, with a heel-hand strike to the face, smashed the Pawnee's nose, driving him back a couple of steps. A spinning back kick to the solar plexus drove the wind from Strong Bear dropped him for good. The crowd roared its approval as the Pawnee writhed on the ground, trying to get his wind back. His pain was overshadowed by the rage he felt.

Later, as the feast began, Bryan and White Bull gave an impressive demonstration of their martial arts skills. They were wildly cheered by all the spectators. While they were seated near the chief, he leaned forward and spoke to the two, entreating them to teach his warriors the martial skills they had demonstrated. It was agreed that they would meet the next day and discuss this in detail.

THE QUEST CONTINUES

The day after the harvest festival, Bryan and the professor were discussing their options. Both of them agreed that they should attempt to find the reasons and the methods for and by which they arrived in this place, but they were not quite sure how to proceed. They couldn't find any commonality in their background or geographical beginnings that would make them believe that they were intended to be together in this adventure.

"Maybe we are not the only ones who are here!" suggested Bryan. "It could be that we are only a small part of the whole picture."

"That thought had occurred to me too, Bryan," replied the professor. "But who or what is controlling all of this? I have always adhered to the basic Christian tenets, but nothing in my religious studies has prepared me for this. Although, I guess anything is possible to a Supreme Deity."

"The martial arts has lead me to explore Buddhism, particularly Zen, where the beliefs are of everything being in balance...you know, black and white, good and evil, right and left, yin and yang. I don't quite see how our situation fits into that unless we are here to balance out something."

"That could be, but what? I think that this needs a little more research. Let's consult with the Pawnee shaman. Maybe he can shed some light on the matter."

The shaman of the Skidi people was old, like Many Moons, his seamed, weather-beaten face showed the evidence of many years. His lodge was near the edge of the village and marked by the trappings of his calling. There were gourd rattles, eagle bone whistles, and bags of medicine talismans hanging from the walls and ceiling. A pungent aroma of burning herbs hung in the thick, dark air.

Bryan and the professor were offered seats by the medicine fire, which was kept burning in the center of the lodge. After the pipe ceremony, the old man's black eyes rested on Bryan.

"You are troubled, Pale Man," he stated. "You want to know why you came to the Cheyenne and now the Skidi people, but you do not know how to seek the answer."

The professor translated for Bryan, though the old man had signed as he spoke, and Bryan got the gist of the statement

Bryan had ceased to be amazed at the insight of these Native American shamans after his months at the side of Many Moons, but the revelation by this Skidi wise man was a little startling.

"You have read my thoughts, wise one," said Bryan, with the professor repeating in Pawnee.

"No, I have been visited by a spirit who told me of your coming and that of this pale shaman here," he said, indicating the professor. "Your coming has been foretold for many years now, even before my time. The spirits have told us of the pale men who would come among the people of the plains, bringing us the knowledge of planting and other ways to improve our ways."

"We seek to know what brought us here and how," interjected the professor.

"The spirits called up by the shamans of many peoples have called you here. It is our destiny to better the lot of our people through magic and the powers of the spirit world. Each of us is trained to summon the spirits to help. You are part of the response we have received after years of repeated requests," said the shaman.

"Yes, but why us?" asked Bryan after the professor had relayed this.

The old man went on, "You each have special skills which the people need. It is your destiny to travel among the tribes, teaching us your ways...of planting and of war."

The conversation continued along the same lines for a while, Bryan and the professor learning that legends passed down from shaman to shaman had foretold the coming of pale ones who would travel among the people. There would be many years of calling on the spirits by many shamans until one day, the elements would all be in place to bring the pale ones among them. Some interpretations had the pale ones as white buffalo or other pale incarnations. The arrival of the professor and Bryan had shown that they would be men.

Back at the professor's lodge, Bryan and he discussed this new information. Bryan was prone to debunk the whole story, his practical side asserting itself, but the professor, a man of science, was ready to consider all alternatives.

"Bryan," he began, "I have learned that the more knowledge I gather, the more I have to learn. I have also learned not to discount anything because we have only a fractional understanding of our world, let alone the whole universe. Things which seem like magic now will probably turn into ordinary events at some future date after we have studied them and learned."

He went on, "The more I am among these people, learning about their ways and their coexistence with their environment, the more I accept their beliefs as factually based."

"What are you saying we should do, Professor?" inquired Bryan.

"When in Rome," he began, "while we are in this world, we should accept the ways and beliefs of these people. They arrived at these conclusions after many years of survival and not just a little bit of studying their environment. Can the Western mind understand the ways of the fakirs in India or the firewalkers or any of the other phenomena of our own time and world? There is just too much that cannot be explained by conventional means...conventional to us, anyway."

"Yeah, but where do we go from here?" asked Bryan.

"We follow the advice of both of our shamans. We travel among the peoples, teaching, training...all the while we are looking for the answers to our dilemma."

Later that night, with Strong Woman snuggled against his back, Bryan thought about what the professor had said about their mutual destiny. He reflected on his life for the past half year, the personal fulfillment he realized with his teaching of martial arts that conversely assured more peace amongst The People and the hostiles who threatened them. Maybe the professor was right. Maybe they had been brought here to this time and place to help the advance of all the peoples they contacted. Maybe there were others like them, with similar skills, others who had been drawn here much like Bryan and the professor. Was it possible that this was part of the grand design by the Creator? Is this the explanation of other mysteries of history? The Great Pyramids in Egypt and of the Inca, Mayan, and Aztec civilizations. Was this the explanation for great men who had risen from among the people to lead and advise when there was a great need? Men like Thomas Jefferson, Benjamin Franklin, the Adamses, Washington, and the few others who made the USA possible?

With these thoughts as he faded in to sleep, Bryan was content with his lot. He was well equipped to prosper in this world. He had the love of a great woman, the friendship of some good men, and the whole world to explore, assisting people with his skills and opening the door for the professor to do the same. Life was good and life was full.

Bryan MacKay was more contented than he had ever been in his life. He was drowsily aware that something had disturbed his sleep…a troubling dream, yet what did he have to be troubled about? He was snuggled in a soft, warm pallet, covered with a buffalo robe, and the love of his life was pressed softly against his back. She had whispered in his ear before they had dropped off for the night that she was quite sure that she was pregnant with their first child. Bryan was amongst friends and allies in the Skidi Pawnee camp, and his life was fulfilling. He sleepily reviewed the past six months in his mind.

By forces he still didn't comprehend, Bryan had dozed off in his dentist's chair while Dr. Bob intoned the phrases to induce the mesmeric state he used for minor dental work instead of an anesthetic. He had awakened, naked, in an unfamiliar locale on a far hillside in a different time. In time, he had discovered that he was in the pre-Columbian discovery period of the Great American West. He had come among The People, as the Cheyenne called themselves, had found friendship, love, and an outlet for all the skills he had developed as a martial artist, adept in the art of karate, a US Army Special Operations officer, and a survivalist of some skill…quite literally, a man out of sync with his time and place…but no more!

Bryan had militarily prepared the warriors of the first clan group he had come among, then among the young men of the other clans, by teaching karate and military tactics. Rather than initiating war between The People and their enemies, it was bringing about a period of peace after the word of their prowess had spread. Now Bryan was on a quest to find out the reasons behind his being where he had found himself, a quest initiated by his mentor, the shaman, Many Moons.

Accompanied by his love, Strong Woman; her brother and Bryan's best friend in any world, Strong Bull; and the Pawnee girl captive, Talks Fast, Bryan had traveled west to the Pawnee, Talks Fast's home village. Then on to where they connected with another spirit traveler to this time, the professor who was residing with another Pawnee clan. Along the way, they had thwarted a raid by the hostile Omaha, endearing themselves to their hosts, and White Bull and Talks Fast had become betrothed.

Like Bryan, the professor had been drawn to this time and place to use his skills as an agronomist to improve the farming skills and yields of the Pawnee nation. He and Bryan had discussed the possibilities of them being part of some central plan of providing their skills to emerging civilizations, much as they surmised has been happening throughout recorded time. It was the professor's contention that it wasn't chance that brought spurts of human development, but people brought from different times and places to where there was a great need for their intelligence, training, and special skills. The professor was fond of pointing to historical characters like Benjamin Franklin and Thomas Jefferson as proof of his theory.

The two products of the twentieth century were beginning to hatch a plan whereby Bryan and his friends would travel from tribe to tribe spreading their message, then bringing in the professor to teach these people how to be better farmers. Bryan's martial skills being the path to peace amongst the tribes and the professor's teachings bringing the freedom from a hunter-gatherer, nomadic lifestyle, to permanent villages of the farmer. The increase in leisure time would allow the development of the arts and sciences of the people.

Bryan and the professor were sure that they were not the only people to be brought to this time and place, that there were others scattered amongst the American Indians bringing their skills to help develop written languages, metallurgy, animal husbandry, and the other necessities of developing civilizations.

On the previous day, the harvest festival of the Pawnee, a day of athletic and martial games and feasting, had interrupted their planning. The karate demonstration put on by Bryan and White Bull had impressed their hosts as had White Bull's meeting and defeating of the Pawnee, Strong Bear, in Indian wrestling. On the next day, they were to develop their detailed plan to expand the teaching of their skills.

HOME AGAIN

Bryan had begun to slip back into sleep in the predawn hour, pushing the troubling dream from his mind, but there was a nagging voice in his ear...

"Nine, eight, seven... You will begin to awaken... Six, five, four... You are becoming more aware of your surroundings..."

He became conscious of his head against the soft pads of the headrest and his arms resting on the arms of the chair.

"You will begin to awaken and at the count of one you will be totally awake... Three, two, and one!"

The glare of the lamp almost obscured Dr. Bob's smiling face above Bryan's head.

"How does that feel?" said the dentist, probing the front tooth with a rubber-gloved finger. "Any tenderness?" The cotton pads were being removed from Bryan's mouth, and there was a surge of cool water, eliminating the dryness caused by their insertion. The dental assistant began to raise the chair into a normal sitting position. When he was upright, she removed the clip-on paper bib from around his neck and pushed back the tray of tools on their swivel arm so that he could exit the elaborate dental chair.

Bryan swiveled his legs to the floor and moved to rise. He was totally disoriented. Moments before, he was snuggled in his pallet with Strong Woman against his back, warm and comfortable. Now he was back in his former life in Jasper, Pennsylvania, having just undergone the repair on his front tooth. His tongue felt the rough edges of the dental material.

"You'll probably feel a little different for a while," said Dr. Bob, who was also one of Bryan's karate students in the dojo where he conducted classes nearly every evening. An uncontrolled elbow in a tournament the previous Saturday, a rare occurrence in higher rank competition, had chipped the tooth.

"Different doesn't describe my feelings," Bryan replied. "What I was feeling before you awoke me was very real, more real in fact, than my feelings right now."

"Not at all uncommon," the dentist replied. "Often the imagined experiences can be very realistic." The dentist continued, "Most of my patients are a little pale after I work on them, but you aren't, in fact you look like your skin is darker. Maybe you are a bit flushed."

A feeling of great despair came over the young man. What he had experienced couldn't have been a hypnotic dream. It involved months and months of living with The People, training the young men, being mentored by the old shaman, developing the strong friendship with

White Bull, and most important, falling in love with Strong Woman.

"Go home and take a nap, B-Man. Then you'll feel better. See you at the dojo tonight, right?

Bryan mumbled some response and made his way out of the dental office in the medical building. He sought his car in the parking lot, after what seemed like a long search because in his mind, months had passed, and he couldn't remember where he had parked. This in itself was odd because Bryan had a very orderly mind and didn't misplace or lose things.

All the way home in his Jeep CJ, his mind couldn't shake the despair he felt about the dream or whatever it was. It had been so very real, but now...here he was in Jasper, Pennsylvania, pulling into the driveway of the small house he had bought shortly after obtaining the teaching position at the high school.

He made his way into the bedroom and stripped off his clothing and went into the bathroom to relieve himself before taking Dr. Bob's advice about a nap. Staring back from the mirror was a face that was definitely his. His color was a little darker, but that was probably a result of the hypnosis effecting his perceptions or something, he thought. He washed his hands then turned to leave the bathroom, glancing at his full-length image in the mirror on the back of the door. Suddenly, he stopped. There was a vivid red scar just below his ribs on his right side! That hadn't been there before the dental visit! The experience wasn't a dream. It must have been real. He recalled the fight with Many Coups and the wound to his side by his knife blade... Now he was really confused.

His legs felt rubbery, so he sat down on the toilet seat to address his confusion. He had been living with The People! Strong Woman and White Bull were real... as were Many Moons and Faces West and all the others he had come to know in whatever other place where he had been. How had he come to be back and why? More importantly, how could he return to Strong Woman and the life he had been living?

BRYAN IS MISSING

Strong Woman awoke with the feeling that something was amiss. Bryan was gone from their bed, probably had gone to relieve himself, she thought, but there was still seemed to be a disquieting pall hanging in the lodge. She rose quickly and donned her clothes. Looking around, she saw Bryan's shirt and leggings still piled neatly beside their pallet.

She emerged from the lodge, being careful not to make any noise so as not to awaken White Bull and Talks A Lot. The camp was still dark, but the eastern horizon was painted with a hint of brightness, a sign that dawn was imminent. There was no movement in the village other than a few camp dogs. The sounds of stirrings in other lodges indicated that others were awakening and preparing for the day.

Strong Woman returned to the lodge. She knelt by the fire-pit and stirred the coals with a stick until she exposed some glowing embers on which she placed a small amount of tinder. When that flamed up, she added some small sticks, then a few larger ones. The lodge brightened with the light from the fire, and she then went to her brother's side and awakened him with a shake.

"Bry-Yan is gone," she told him.

"Maybe he's making water?" replied White Bull.

"No, I checked and there is no sign of him...and his clothing is still here."

White Bull arose and dressed quickly. Talks A Lot awoke, disturbed by her husband's movement. White Bull explained the situation to his new bride, and then he left the wood and earthen lodge to look for his friend.

Most of the village was still at rest, the people tired from the grueling games at the harvest festival the day before, but there was noise of activity in the professor's lodge when White Bull approached. He scratched at the door and waited politely for a response. Shortly, the professor's wife opened the portal and invited him in. The white man was seated across the small cook fire from the doorway and signed for White Bull to be seated.

"Bry-Yan is missing," began the Cheyenne. "He took nothing, not even his clothing. Maybe he has returned to the world from whence he came?"

"I don't know about that, White Bull, because I don't understand exactly how we both came to be in the place, but that is a distinct possibility. Maybe the spirits felt his duty was done...or the call from his home pulled him back. I think we should consult with the shaman in this village, and if he cannot help us, we should go back to your village and consult with your shaman, the one who called Bryan to this place."

"I will get Strong Woman and Talks A Lot and meet you at the lodge of the holy man," said the warrior. He rose and left the professor's lodge.

A short while later, the four of them gathered at the shaman's lodge. After much discussion with the holy man, it was decided that White Bull and the women should return to their village and seek the assistance of Many Moons, their shaman, who was the only one who knew what spells and spirits had been invoked to bring Bryan here.

They returned to their lodge and packed their backpacks. Spotted Calf was told, and he detailed four warriors to accompany them in case there were still some Omaha in the area.

Within an hour, they had departed to the east. They had at least ten days of travel before them, if they hurried.

BRYAN DEVELOPS A PLAN

Bryan's orderly mind was focused on his problem—how to return to Strong Woman and his friends. He reasoned that it was Many Moons calling him through the Spirit World that pulled him into their time and place. He had to reconnect with Many Moons in any way he could. In his time with The People and the brief time among the Pawnee, Bryan had learned that the Indian peoples were very mystical. They had strong beliefs about their creator and the spirit world, beliefs that seemed to be upheld by the events of their lives and the harmony in which they lived with the flora and fauna of their world. Mysticism was very much a part of their everyday lives. Never very spiritual in his former life, Bryan had come to accept and believe in the spirit world of the Indian.

It was his thought that maybe an Indian shaman could help him reconnect, but where could he find one? The nearest reservation or Indian settlement was a couple hundred miles away in the Southern Tier of New York, the Seneca Nation of the Iroquois near Salamanca...or maybe it would be better to go west to the Cheyenne reservation. He recalled that there was a major Cheyenne encampment somewhere in Montana and another in Oklahoma. He figured he had better go the library and do a little research, then plan a trip. First, however, he would go to his parents' house and tell them of his experience. He wanted his father's input on the whole situation.

It was mid afternoon when Bryan pulled his Jeep into his parents' driveway. The garage door was open, and he could see both of their cars inside. He entered through the kitchen door without knocking though he had paused and had almost scratched at the portal as in the manner of The People. Little things like this kept reminding him that his life with Strong Woman had been a reality.

His mom was at the kitchen table reading a woman's magazine and drinking a cup of coffee. She looked up and smiled.

"Hi, Bry. Can you stay for dinner?"

"No, Mom, I just want to talk to you and Dad. Where is he?"

"Sounds serious," she said with a smile. "He's in the living room in his favorite chair, where else."

Then both went into the living room, where Bryan's dad was parked in the old lounger reading a news magazine. He looked up when they entered.

"Hi there, son. What's going on with you?"

"Dad, I need to talk to you and Mom about something, and I need your unbiased opinion, undivided attention."

"Okay, you've got it."

Bryan began his tale. "I know that you are going to find all this hard to believe, but this is all very real. As you know, I went to Dr. Bob today to have my chipped tooth repaired." Bryan launched into his story about waking up on the far hill. His father listened intently while his mother sat on the couch nearby, an incredulous look on her face.

As Bryan proceeded with the story, both his parents sat quietly, raptly absorbing what their elder child was telling them. Bryan had always been a truthful and thoughtful son. They had never had any cause to question whether his feet were planted firmly on the ground. This tale they were hearing was wild, impossible, but someone they had never doubted was telling it.

It was nearly an hour later when Bryan paused in recounting his experiences in the nether world. There was silence for a moment, and then his father spoke, "That's quite a story, son, quite a lot to absorb."

Bryan stood and pulled up his shirt. The vivid scar was very evident across his ribs.

"This wasn't here when I sat down in Dr. Bob's chair, Dad. Also, I have acquired a total body tan. I was doubting my 'dream' too, but this evidence sort of refutes the doubts." Bryan went on, "Additionally, I seem to have acquired a vocabulary of the Cheyenne tongue and learned hand-speak too." He uttered a couple of phrases in the language of The People while using his hands to sign the same sentences.

Bryan's mother immediately began to respond emotionally. Her first thought was the potential loss of her elder son, and she was resistant. His dad was more logical but had much the same thoughts. Bryan explained that he would miss being near them as well as how much he loved Strong Woman and how much The People needed him. They discussed the matter, at times heatedly, for what seemed like hours. Finally, his parents seemed to understand his need.

His father said, "I don't doubt you, son. It's just a lot to absorb. My initial reaction is to advise you that if this is all real and you can find some way to do it, you should return to where you were. It sounds like you have found yourself there. Your mother and I have always worried that you would never be fulfilled, never satisfied with your life in Jasper. Our main concern is for your happiness. Though we selfishly want you near us, we only want the best for you."

Bryan's mother chimed in, "Your father is right, Bryan. We want only the best for you. As a mother, I want you close. I want to see you marry, and I want to see my grandchildren. But that doesn't seem to be possible now. I hope that there will be some way to communicate back to us, if you do find your way back to Strong Woman."

Bryan knew how hard it was for his parents to be supportive, particularly his mother. His only consolation was that his younger brother, Jason, was still nearby at the university. Promising to return for dinner, Bryan left for the library.

At the local library, he used one of their computers to do a data search on the Cheyenne Nation, looking for historical and geographical information about their origins and movement from the Great Lakes region to the Great Plains. He was guessing at the timing to be shortly before or just after the arrival of the first white men to the Western Hemisphere toward the end of the fifteenth century. He had seen no evidence of horses or of the great horse culture of the plains during his time with The People and the Pawnee.

His research disclosed that the earliest migration away from the Great Lakes came about when the larger, stronger Sioux tribe had moved into the lands of The People. This migration of the first bands of Cheyenne came about 1500 CE, but it was nearly 150 years later before those who resisted the push gave in and moved west to an area around the Red River in North Dakota, a branch of which was named the Cheyenne River in later years. The first Cheyenne-speaking people on the Plains were called the Sutaio and had established themselves on the plains between the head river and the Black Hills in what is now South Dakota. Bryan figured out that the timing on these events was fuzzy at best because much of the information had been handed down verbally from generation to generation of The People.

The Pawnee, he learned, were made up of four independent bands, each of which was divided into permanent villages, the basic social unit, which were made up of large, dome-shaped earthen lodges. They were much more populous than the Cheyenne, with maybe three times as many people, but their bands were autonomous and seldom came together other than socially. These bands were spread over the region around the Platte River.

Bryan did some research into the Paiute and Shoshone peoples since he hoped to be traveling to their lands if he managed to get back to Strong Woman and White Bull. He also located a directory for Texas A&M and found Charles Branson listed in the School of Agriculture. An internet search on the library PC pulled up newspapers from a year before. In one from Bryan-College Station, Texas, was the headline and article about Branson being missing from his home. A couple of follow-up articles indicated that he was not found. Interest had faded, and there were no more follow-ups.

A plan was beginning to form in Bryan's mind. He would travel west to the region where he believed his band of Cheyenne lived. He would search the area to try and find the specific locations he had become familiar with during his time with The People. Once located, he would camp there until he was able to reconnect with Many Moons or Strong Woman and be drawn back to their time and place. Before he did that, he would locate a Cheyenne shaman on their reservation to see if he could obtain assistance or at least information on how to go about his quest.

Lame Deer, Montana, is the headquarters for the Northern Cheyenne Reservation, and that would be Bryan's first destination, but first, he had some other things to take resolve.

At dinner with his parents, Bryan laid out his plan. He explained that he would be heading for Montana in a few days after he had taken care of all personal business—a leave of absence from Jasper High School, arranging for his karate dojo to be run by his sempai in his absence with all dues payments to be deposited with Bryan's bank, setting up automatic payments to be made from his checking, savings, and retirement accounts to satisfy his small mortgage and other expenses. Although he hoped to remain with Strong Woman, if he was successful in returning to her, he didn't want to dissolve his current life until he knew for sure. He would also set up a will so that if he didn't return in the allotted period, his parents could dispose of his possessions and use the funds for his brother, Jason. The details of his plan convinced his parents that Bryan had thought things through and was committed to his course of action.

At his dojo that night, Bryan threw himself into the training. While the junior students were led in exercised and kata by one of his senior students, a first-degree black belt, Bryan worked with his senior students on advanced kata. Dr. Bob was in this class.

After the class, while the other students where changing back into street clothes, he and the dentist had a private conversation. Bryan told his sempai that he was going to be gone for an indefinite period and got Dr. Bob's commitment to look after the business affairs of the dojo. Also, he wanted the sempai to allocate the teaching of classes to the other senior students. Bryan went on to say that he was leaving a letter with his attorney that was to be given to Dr. Bob if Bryan hadn't returned to Jasper in a specific period of time.

The sempai was stunned. He asked for an explanation, and Bryan, feeling that his friend deserved one, launched into a brief description of his experience in the Spirit World while under hypnosis for the tooth repair.

"I know you are going to think I'm crazy," he began, "but I'm not. I found something wonderful, and I have to try and find it again, or I'll really be crazy."

He spent about half an hour telling Dr. Bob about The People, Strong Woman, White Bull, the Pawnee, the professor, and the months he had spent on the Great Plains. He showed the scar on his ribs, still fresh enough to be pink against his very tanned skin. At the conclusion of his tale, he had the dentist convinced.

"Bry, maybe if you were able to produce a mesmeric state through self-hypnosis, you could go back? What do you think?" said Dr. Bob. "I can teach you self-hypnosis and then put you under and give you a post-hypnotic suggestion that will enable you to achieve this state without me."

"I'm willing to try anything. When can you do it?"

"Right now. It won't take long."

After the dojo had cleared for the evening. Bryan shut off most of the lights, and he and his sempai retired to the back room where Bryan sat back in an old easy chair while Dr. Bob sat in a straight-backed chair beside him.

"I want you to close your eyes and relax," Dr. Bob began.

Thirty minutes later, they were done. Dr. Bob had given Bryan the post-hypnotic suggestion that when he closed his eyes and crossed any two fingers of his left hand, he would relax and enter a mesmeric state, his mind freed from earthly constraints. The dentist suggested that he try it while alone this evening, but maybe Bryan's plan to return to the Great Plains region of his experiences was more valid.

THE QUEST BEGINS

Within three days, Bryan had concluded his business and personal business and was ready to start west. He packed his Jeep with survival gear, his old Remington Model 788 .308 hunting rifle, his S&W Model 29 .44 magnum, four boxes of ammunition for each, several hunting knives, a camp axe, and assorted camp cooking utensils. He didn't expect to do any hunting, but he wanted to be prepared for anything.

The Auto Club had supplied him with detailed maps of the trip and the area of his quest. He had drawn two thousand dollars in cash from his account, had an ATM card in case he needed more. The gas tank on the Jeep was full, and there were two five-gallon jerry-cans full of gas in the racks on the back. He had said his good-byes to his parents the night before and had called his brother. He was leaving it to his parents to tell Jason the story when he came home on his next school break. It was 5:00a.m. when he locked up his little house and hit the road.

The night before, he had tried, for the third time, to reach Strong Woman while in a mesmeric state. Though he was able to achieve self-hypnosis, he wasn't able to free himself from the present time and return to his love and his life with The People. He wasn't discouraged; however, he was actually encouraged because he had felt something, some slipping of his bonds, before awakening.

It was his intent to take the highway southwest out of Jasper, pick up The Pennsylvania Turnpike and head due west. He would exit the Turnpike where Interstate 70 split off, near New Stanton, to avoid the traffic in Pittsburgh, plus that of Cleveland and Chicago. I-70 would take him across Ohio, through Columbus, skirting Dayton on the north side and into Indiana. West of Indianapolis, he would pick up I-74 and cross Illinois on this route, reaching Interstate 80 near the Iowa state line. He figured he could make it that far the first day, a little over seven hundred miles by his calculations. If he made good time and had no problems, he might even make it to Des Moines, another 150 or so miles, before stopping for the night. The Jeep was nearly new and in good shape, and his tires were good, and he was young and energetic. Bryan anticipated no problems. He had packed a large thermos of coffee, a cooler of bottled water and energy drinks and a lot of healthy snacks. He planned on stopping only for gas and in rest stops to relieve his bladder.

The first day of the journey went without any special events. Bryan stopped for the night near Iowa City. He had eaten at a truck stop a couple of hours earlier, so he just sought a motel at an off-ramp on the west side of the college town. The room was large enough that he was able to stretch out, do some basic techniques from a horse stance and several nearly stationary kata before showering and bedding down for the night. Before first light, he was up and checked out of the motel. He filled his thermos with fresh coffee in the motel office and then hit the road. He chewed on a piece of jerky as he drove.

Four hours later, he came to Interstate 29 and took it north for Sioux City. He crossed into South Dakota on I-29, and an hour later, he was in Sioux Falls where he stopped for lunch. He had bought a prepaid cell phone before he left home, which he now used to call his parents' home. His mother answered, and he gave her an update on his travels. They chatted briefly, both avoiding any discussion of Bryan's quest or what the future might bring.

After a brief lunch, Bryan now headed west on Interstate 90 toward Rapid City. An uneventful six hours later, he exited the interstate near Sturgis on US Highway 212. He stopped for dinner in a small town just inside the Montana border. The small family restaurant was clean and neat. Bryan treated himself to a steak with all the trimmings, wishing all the time he ate that it was buffalo hump ribs and Strong Woman was eating with him. Bryan was now less than two hundred miles from his destination, so he stopped for the night in a clean, comfortable motel.

MANY MOONS CALLS

Strong Woman and her party reached their home village in the late afternoon after ten days of trekking across the plains from the Pawnee village. There was little activity as most of the men were hunting, and the women were putting together the evening meals. After leaving their packs and Talks A Lot with her mother, White Bull and she went to see Many Moons. The sides of his lodge were pulled up due to the warmth of the day, so the shaman saw them coming. They were invited into the lodge and waved into seats across from the old man.

"I see that Bry-Yan isn't with you," said the shaman, without any of the usual formalities.

"He disappeared while we were with the Skidi," replied White Bull. "We think he may have been called back to his world."

Strong Woman spoke, "We want to bring him back. The Skidi shaman suggested that you are our best hope."

Many Moons could see the anguish on her face though her voice was low and respectful.

"I believe that Bry-Yan's work here isn't done. We will cleanse ourselves and free our minds. We will enter the Spirit World together, and maybe the strength of our call and our need will bring him back to us," replied the old shaman.

After preparing the sweat lodge for their cleansing, the three of them entered, stripped off their clothing, and seated themselves around the small fire, which was heating the rocks for the steam. Strong Woman used two sticks to move heated rocks from the edge of the fire to the water filled buffalo stomach caldron hung from a nearby rack. The hissing steam immediately filled the small dome-shaped lodge. Sweat glistened on their bodies in the dim light offered by the small blaze. The air became moist and stifling. Breathing shallowly through their noses, the trio sat quietly for a while, sweat pouring off their bodies and soaking the earth beneath them. Many Moons began a low chanting, calling on the Great Spirit to purify them, to remove the poisons from their minds and bodies so that they could send out their call to Bry-Yan. Strong Woman felt her spirit soar, freed from earthly restraints. Bry-Yan filled her mind as his seed was filling her womb. She could almost feel his physical presence.

After what seemed to be only a few minutes, but in fact was more than an hour, the shaman stopped chanting. After a brief period, he rose and opened the door of the sweat lodge allowing cooling air to bathe their bodies. They left the lodge and entered the adjacent stream to wash the perspiration from their bodies, dressed, and returned to the lodge of Many Moons. With their bodies cleansed by the steam, their stomachs empty of food, and their minds freed by the meditation, they were ready to begin their calling out to Bry-Yan. The shaman gathered his mystic tools, and they departed for the nearby knoll.

Night had fallen during their cleansing steam bath, but the old man unerringly led them to the crest where they seated themselves facing the direction of the rising sun. From his medicine bag, the shaman produced small, dried disks of cactus root. They placed these under their tongues and sat quietly waiting for the mind-freeing hallucinogen to take effect. This was a new experience to both Strong Woman and her brother, but not unfamiliar to the old shaman, who had acquired the disks from another of his kind who had traded for them with a Comanche shaman. The furry cactus was native to the lands far to the South and was not available amongst the northern plains peoples, except through trade with their southern neighbors.

Contrary to popular modern belief, the American Indians were not constantly at war, and there was a flourishing trade among the tribes. In this manner, medicinal herbs, crudely smelted copper, furs, and other goods reached into areas where they weren't produced. Pottery arts were developed among the people living in permanent villages along the Mississippi and Missouri Rivers and in the pueblos of the Southwest, while the nomadic peoples tanned the hides of buffalo, elk, deer, antelope, wolves, and other fur-bearing animals. Near the present day Upper Peninsula of Michigan were mineral deposits including raw copper. These items were the trade goods that travel regularly from their origination area on regular routes throughout the Indian world.

Gradually, Strong Woman became less aware of her body and more aware of her surroundings. After a while, she experienced a feeling of lightness, and then it seemed like she was looking down at her seated body and those of her two companions. She felt the shaman's presence and soon that of her brother, White Bull. The shaman began to chant softly, the call haunting and persuasive. It seemed that Many Moons, White Bull, and Strong Woman had melded their minds. The shaman's voice rose, calling to Bry-Yan, their Spirit Warrior, to return to them.

Gradually, she became aware of another spiritual presence... It was Bry-Yan. Because their spirits were linked, she knew the others felt him too. Together, they called to her mate, their Spirit Warrior. Bry-Yan was aware of them but only barely. The shaman's chanting intensified, but after a short time, the image of Bry-Yan began to fade.

Strong Woman was not conscious of the passage of time until the horizon turned pale yellow, heralding the arrival of the sun. She became aware of her surroundings, the hard ground under her, the aches in her legs and back from the physical stress she endured during the travels in the Spirit World. All their spirits returned to their bodies, and they began to stir. The old shaman was the first to speak.

"We made contact with Bry-Yan's spirit tonight. It wasn't strong, but we must continue to call him every evening until he comes to us."

Strong Woman was both sad and uplifted. She had felt her man's spirit and knew he felt her, but he was still in the other world. She could hardly wait until that evening to try again. She knew he would be with her again. It was their destiny.

A CALL IS HEARD

The dream was very vivid and woke him. He had seen
Strong Woman, White Bull, and Many Moons seated
on the hilltop where he and Many Moons had sat on
a vision quest so many months ago. He could feel their
spirits summoning him to them. He tried to reach out,
but his arms were leaden, and when he moved toward
them, it was if he was chest deep in sucking muck that
was sapping his strength. Try as he might, he couldn't free
himself, and his love and his friends began to fade from
view as if a fog had rolled in.

The bedding was soaked with sweat and wrapped
around his legs as if he had been trying to run. He freed
his legs and rolled to the edge of the bed. After a moment,
he rose, went to the sink, and splashed cold water on his
face. Fully awake, he sat in the worn easy chair in the
motel room and pondered the dream. Was it a real spirit
call, or was it just a dream? He couldn't tell. He wished
he could counsel with Many Moons about how to get
back to The People. All he could think of was to repeat
the circumstances of his previous journey to them, under

hypnosis, and called by the spirit of the Shaman and he prayed that would work.

He rose and went to the window and looked out. In the predawn light, he could see his Jeep in the parking stall just outside the door. There were a few other cars in spaces around the circular drive, all of which had been there when Bry-Yan had checked in late last night. He made a decision to continue on toward Lame Deer and then use that as a base of operations to seek the summer camp of The People as he recalled it from his hunting and explorations while with them. One landmark that stood out in his mind was the buffalo leap of the successful hunt in which he had participated. This was a sharp drop-off into a deep ravine with low hills bordering the path to the edge. He felt sure that this would not have changed much despite the passage of time since he was there with The People.

A short time later, Bryan, showered, shaved, and dressed, stowed his bag in the back of the Jeep and was pulling onto the highway, heading west toward the Cheyenne Reservation and Lame Deer. He had about a three-hour trip, and that would put him there about nine o'clock in the morning. He didn't know where to start, but he figured if he asked a few people, he could get the lay of the land. Also, he might be able to locate a Chamber of Commerce or Real Estate office where he could get some detailed maps.

The disquieting dream of last night wouldn't leave his mind. Tonight, he promised himself he would use self-hypnosis and attempt to enter the Spirit World and contact Strong Woman, White Bull, and Many Moons, all of whom he had sensed in the dream. The more he though about it, the more real the dream was; in fact, he could remember every detail, and he didn't think that was true of dreams. He hoped it was a real contact from them. He wanted to be as close to the location of the summer camp area before attempting this, as he didn't want to travel far with no clothes or food and have to go through the whole survival experience once again.

Thinking about clothing, tools, and weapons brought to mind some of his conversations with Many Moons after he had learned some of the language of the people. He had wondered why he arrived as he had, with nothing but his birthday suit. The shaman had thought about that and finally concluded that nothing could be transported through the Spirit World that was not of the time of the destination. Even though it may not be from that specific place it had to be from that time or earlier. Maybe if Bryan could find items that came from the late fifteenth century or before, he could take them with him. It would be worth a try.

He arrived in Lame Deer about nine o'clock as he had anticipated. He was going to fill up his gas tank before anything else, but he spotted a real estate office on the main drag and pulled into the diagonal parking space in front. Alighting from the Jeep, he entered the office and was greeted by a bright, smiling lady. She was dusky skinned, raven haired, and dressed in casual business attire.

"May I help you?" was her inquiry.

"I'm looking for detailed maps of the area, the whole reservation, if you have them," said Bryan.

"Well, I have some local maps of Lame Deer and several of the other communities, but it sounds like you want a county map or maybe a topographical map. You'll have to go to the county offices to get those, but I have a pretty good map of the reservation you can have." She paused, then went on, "Is there something in particular you're looking for? Maybe I can help?"

"I'm looking for some old landmarks," said Bryan. "Researching for a paper I'm doing for school." He stretched the truth a bit. "I'm studying the early Cheyenne people, how they lived, and all that," he went on, a little more truthful now. "You know, before the White Man came and corrupted them," he added with a friendly grin.

"Well, there are some old sites around here," responded the real estate lady. There are some early sites where relics have been found and then there's the buffalo leap. You should get someone from the reservation headquarters to help locate those for you. Some of the sites have archeological teams from the U of M or MSU there, and you can probably visit them, talk to the team leaders."

At his request, the real estate lady told him how to get to the tribal headquarters, and Bryan left with a reservation map, which appeared quite detailed.

As he gassed up at a convenience store just down the street from the real estate office, a battered pickup truck pulled to the pumps on the other side of the island. There were two women and several children of varying ages in the back, apparently Indian from their looks. The women had on denim skirts and colorful cotton blouses, and the kids were in jeans and T-shirts, all worn but clean.

An older man, with a face like creased, well-tanned leather, got out of the cab and prepared to fill the gas tank of the truck. He was wearing a dark wide-brimmed hat with a creased, peaked crown, western-style shirt, blue jeans, and well-worn cowboy boots. He spoke to the women in the back.

Bryan realized that the man was using the tongue of The People. The idiom was different than he knew, but it was Cheyenne. He was telling one of the women to get him some Bugler tobacco when she went in to prepay for the gas. The woman heaved herself erect, climbed over the tailgate, and started for the convenience store. The man waited for the pump to turn on before he turned on the nozzle.

Bryan spoke to him in Cheyenne, "My brother, where may I find a shaman?"

The man was very startled hearing the Tongue coming from the big man at the next pump. He looked at him for a moment and then replied, "Where did you learn the language of The People? Your accent is strange, but you know the words."

"A friend taught me," Bryan replied. "I have a number of friends among The People, but they are far from here."

"Southern Cheyenne?" asked the Indian. "I have some friends on the Cheyenne-Arapaho Reservation in Oklahoma, but they talk much the same as we Northern Cheyenne, maybe a little slang difference, but the same."

"No, they live in a much different place. I am looking for some information on old sites around here, but I also need to talk to a shaman. Can you help me, please?"

The pump had turned on, and the Indian began to fill his gas tank. "There is a shaman living out on Spotted Creek Road," he began. "Go south out of town, then turn right on Spotted Creek. Name's Charlie Littlebear, an old geezer. His shack is about four miles on the left. Hard to miss. It's the only place that far out."

Bryan thanked the man and then went into the convenience store to get the change back from the twenty he had left before pumping the gas. He bought a couple of liter bottles of water, then left. He checked the rearview mirror as he pulled out of the driveway and saw that the Indian woman had returned and was getting in to the truck bed. The man was standing by the open door, watching the Jeep as it left the station.

A few blocks further, Bryan came to a stop sign and turned left. As he passed the village limits, the blacktop ended, and the road was oiled gravel, or what is laughingly called an improved road on many map keys though this one appeared well maintained and had few potholes. A short distance south of Lame Deer, the road passed over a creek on a metal bridge with a plank bed. The planks rumbled and rattled under the all-terrain tires of the Jeep. Just over the bridge was a rough gravel road to the right, and Bryan turned down it. It meandered along the creek for a ways, now and then passing clapboard shacks or battered-looking trailers on blocks that had little or no signs of habitation. After he had traveled about three miles, he stopped seeing any houses. Suddenly, on a small ridge overlooking the creek, there was a shack. The drive leading up to the house was two tracks worn in the buffalo grass. Bryan topped the small rise and drove into the yard. There was a beat-up Chevy pickup parked near the small, neat-looking house. Underneath a small, shady tree was an old man seated on a bench. Behind him was a pole corral in which a couple of pinto ponies stood lazily, head to tail, swishing flies off each other's faces. The old man looked intently at the Jeep and the big man driving as the SUV came to a stop by the pickup.

Bryan unbuckled his seatbelt and eased out of the Jeep. As he walked toward the seated man, he raised his right hand in the universal sign of peace and then made the sign of greeting an elder. A widening of the old man's eyes was the only sign that he was startled, but he immediately signed back.

"Greetings, Father," began Bryan, "I seek the assistance of a shaman. A man in town directed me here."

The old man spoke back in the Tongue, "Welcome, son. I am Charlie Littlebear, practitioner of the old arts. Forgive me if I am a little surprised as most of the young ones today have forgotten their heritage and the importance of the old ways. What need do you have of a holy man?"

"My mentor, Many Moons, is a shaman of The People. I need to contact him through the spirit world, but I do not know the way."

"I can probably help you, but it involves a cleansing," said Charlie Littlebear. "It is not the way of The People to ask many questions, but I am curious. I have not heard of this shaman, Many Moons. Where is he that you need the spirit world to contact him? Is he with the Great Spirit?"

"He is of another time, Wise One," began Bryan. "I have a story to tell." Bryan launched into an explanation. "Moons ago, I was summoned through the spirit world by Many Moons, a great shaman of The People of an earlier time. I was called to teach martial skills to the warriors of his clan. Before my task was complete and against my will, I was drawn back into this time, and I need to return to finish my task...and there is my woman who is with our child."

"Ah, a Spirit Warrior," said Charlie Littlebear. "Our old ones have many stories of such persons who have helped The People in times of great need. There are many painted records of these Spirit Warriors in the Cheyenne Museum at the reservation headquarters. We even have a few artifacts that may have come from a much earlier time. I can help you, Spirit Warrior, but we must erect a sweat lodge and purify ourselves. Help me erect the lodge, then come back tonight, and we will mind-travel."

He rose, motioned for Bryan to follow him, and went around the house to a shed in back. From within, he took out a canvas bundle wrapped around a number of curved poles. They took the materials to a small flat area near the creek and then they laid out the canvas, poles, and other items. In a short time, a curved frame was erected, over which they stretched the canvas. They then used pegs to fasten down the sides. There was a small slit entry over which was sewn a canvas flap, and there was a smoke hole in the top.

Charlie Littlebear returned to the shed and got a large steel pot with a handle. Together, they collected fist-sized round stones from the creek side. The old man said, "Leave me now, and I will prepare everything for tonight. Go back to town, have a meal, go to our tribal museum, and look at the artifacts I told you of. Be back here about nightfall."

As he walked back to his Jeep in front of the house, he saw an old Indian woman watching him from the back door. How long she had been there, he had no idea, but she watched him come up the slope, then silently disappeared within the house. He got in the Jeep and headed back to Lame Deer.

After a light lunch out of his "backseat pantry," he sought out the Cheyenne Museum at the tribal headquarters. He spent an interesting few hours browsing the displays. There were several painted hides, and though the paint had faded a lot and his knowledge of the symbols was very limited, he could still trace the story of a Spirit Warrior visitation. Of particular interest was the last display, purported to be relics from the ancient past of The People. The display consisted of well-tanned shirt, leggings, breechclout, and moccasins, also a bull hide shield, a flint-tipped spear with a heavy shaft, and a copper knife beside a beaded knife case. The decorative quillwork was intricate, the painting on the shield was decorative too, but both were very faded by time. The leather garments appeared to be in good shape though but creased where they had been folded in storage. The warrior who wore them must have been large because they looked to be Bryan's size.

Toward dusk, Bryan returned to the home of Charlie Littlebear. The old shaman was waiting for him. He had prepared a fire in the sweat lodge and had a pot of water heating on a steel tripod over it. The rocks from the stream were placed around the edges of the fire and must have been heating for a time because one of them had cracked from the heat, probably from internal moisture expansion.

The two men stripped off their clothing, then entered the lodge. Bryan seated himself on the right side of the fire pit while the old man used two sticks to pick up a heated rock and ease it into the pot. Immediately, there was a loud hissing and steam filled the lodge. Bryan closed his eyes and relaxed as the sweat began to pour off his body. He breathed shallowly though his nose, the heated air almost too uncomfortable to bear. Charlie began a low chanting, asking the spirits to cleanse their minds and their bodies before they sought to enter the spirit world. The chanting seemed to fade away in Bryan's mind, which he was trying to focus on his mate, Strong Woman and his friends among The People. After what seemed like a few minutes, though it was much longer, the chanting stopped. After a moment, Charlie Littlebear rose and opened the door flap on the lodge. Cool air washed over their bodies, drying the sweat. Following Charlie, Bryan left the lodge, went to the creek, and immersed himself in the cool, clear water. He felt very refreshed.

"Now we will contact the spirit world," said the shaman. They dressed quickly, and then Bryan followed Charlie up the hillside behind his house to a small flat bench near the crest. They seated themselves facing the direction of the rising sun. Charlie offered Bryan a drink of a strong-smelling liquid from a dark pint bottle he produced from his pocket. Bryan demurred, thinking he didn't need anything to free his mind. The Indian took a healthy swig, capped the bottle, and hid it away. As they sat quietly for a few minutes, waiting for the drug to take effect, Bryan crossed his left fore and middle fingers and began to enter a mesmeric state. Very quickly it seemed the minds of Bryan and the old Cheyenne seemed to merge. The shaman began a low chant, asking the spirits to allow them into the spirit world, to allow them to contact Many Moons and Strong Woman.

Every one of Bryan's senses was cloudy as if he were in a thick, heavy fog. Shortly, the haze began to clear, and he was able to see and sense with great clarity. He felt Charlie Littlebear with him, and they began to look around. A short distance away, they could see three people seated facing them, and they began to move toward the trio. As he approached, Bryan could see that they were Many Moons, White Bull, and the love of his life, Strong Woman. His spirit soared. His elation seeing his wife was so great that he was overcome by both a great strength and a weakness. The strength prevailed, and he moved closer and spoke with her.

"Woman of my life, I have missed you greatly. I wish to be with you always." He could see that Strong Woman was aware of him as were the other two.

"My Spirit Warrior, I call you to me," said the beautiful woman.

"Bry-Yan," began Many Moons, "there is still need of your skills in the lodges of The People, and your wife is with child who will need a father. You have a destiny to fulfill, and we are praying to the Great Spirit to allow you pass through to your family and friends in our place." The old shaman continued, "Our connection is strong, much stronger than on our other contact, and I sense you will join us soon, but it will take more callings to bring you back to us. The holy man spirit with you is pure, and he knows the old ways. He will be able to help you on this journey."

The scene began to fade, and Bryan was almost overcome by the disappointment he felt at not being able to hold his mate. He felt the strength of her spirit and was somewhat comforted by the knowledge he would soon be with her. Soon, he and Charlie Littlebear lost their spirit connection and found themselves seated on the small, flat bench near the crest of the hill behind Charlie's house. The sun was beginning to brighten the eastern sky, so they had been in the spirit world most of the night.

They were both exhausted from their trip and made their way carefully down the slope and back to Charlie's house. His wife, the old woman Bryan had seen in the doorway yesterday, had coffee on the stove and was preparing pancakes on a large griddle over a wood kitchen stove. The aroma of the coffee and grilling food was intoxicating. The woman set two mugs of coffee and a platter of pancakes on the table and then withdrew from the kitchen, leaving the two men to eat and discuss their adventure.

After serving his guest a stack of pancakes, then piling some on a plate for himself, Charlie passed him a jug of homemade syrup. Bryan poured the thick, dark liquid over the top of the stack and passed the jug back. As Charlie poured, he began, "I sense your destiny is with your clan, and you will be able to reach them soon, probably tonight. You didn't pass through last night because you still have things to do here. I'm not quite sure what they are, but we will both work on this, and you may be able to make the journey tonight."

Bryan forked in a huge bite of pancake and reflected a moment as he chewed. "I don't know what I need to do here either, but I'll spend the day getting my house in order and maybe that will take care of my business in this world. I don't know how to thank you for your help."

"Bry-Yan, I am the one to thank you. You are renewing my spirit and giving me faith that the past of my people may be influenced or changed so that our future may be brighter. I have just thought of some preparation I need to make for you. You take care of your business, then come back here to rest before we mind-travel tonight."

They finished the meal and had several more cups of the strong, rich coffee. Neither was inclined to talk about their shared experience, just sat quietly enjoying the coffee and the companionship of a shared experience.

Later, in Lame Deer, Bryan found a storefront office of an attorney and had him draw up a will and power of attorney forms for the transfer of his worldly goods. These he put in an envelope to be left with Charlie Littlebear, along with his Jeep and gear, to be held for his parents to retrieve. He called his parents home, and when his mother answered, he asked her to get his father on the extension. When his dad was listening, he told them what had transpired and what was to happen this evening. He explained that connection had been made to Strong Woman, and he expected to pass through the Spirit World to be with her. He explained that the Jeep and his guns and equipment would be with Charlie Littlebear for them to retrieve at their convenience. They talked for about an hour, sometimes emotional, sometimes calm, but in the end, both his father and mother were supportive of Bryan's quest. His father had one last request.

"Bryan, if there is any way possible, try to get us a message about your life, your wife, and children."

"Dad, the only way I can think of is to leave some record that will be found in this time. I'll try to come up with something or some way to let you know...maybe through Charlie Littlebear."

Back at Charlie's, he and the old shaman sat under the tree and talked a while. The Cheyenne had a package that he told Bryan contained some things they needed for the young man's passage to the past. Bryan made arrangements for Charlie to keep the Jeep and gear for his parents to pick up in the near future. He gave the old man the Remington rifle as a gift, along with the ammunition and a good hunting knife. Charlie tried to remain stoic, but the pleasure in the gift shone in his dark eyes.

"Charlie, I will try to contact you from time to time through the Spirit World. Please call my parents and pass on any information you can." Bryan then gave the Indian the prepaid cell phone into which was programmed his parent's telephone number. The old man promised he would do as requested.

Bryan then pulled his sleeping bag from the back of the Jeep and spread it out under the shady tree and stretched out. His mind was such a jumble of thoughts that, even though very tired, it was some time before he fell asleep.

He awakened shortly before sundown. He and Charlie retired to the sweat lodge to purify for their voyage. After the dousing in the creek after the sweat, they dried, dressed, and headed to the bench on the hillside. Night had fallen, and a myriad of stars filled the sky. The moon hadn't risen, but there was sufficient starlight to navigate their way up the slope.

When the got to the bench, Charlie fumbled around in the dark for a moment, then came to Bryan with his arms full.

"The curator of the museum is my blood kin, and when I told him of your journey, he bade me give these to you." In his arms were the ancient buckskins, shield, spear, and copper knife. "He felt that these may have been yours before our time, and he is just returning them to you."

Bryan was speechless. He knew how much these artifacts must mean to The People, but he also understood the gift to him. He doffed his clothing and pulled on the skins, surprised to find that they fit him quite well. The haft of the spear felt natural in his hands. He stuck the knife case through his belt and seated himself beside Charlie, facing east. Again, the old man swigged from the dark bottle. Bryan crossed two fingers on his left had, closed his eyes, and felt the tension begin to leave his body. Soon the shaman's chanting began, his voice was low, but Bryan felt it in his mind as well.

THE RETURN OF THE SPIRIT WARRIOR

Strong Woman and her brother were seated at either side of the old shaman. They were purified, bodies emptied of food and their minds freed by the peyote tabs. The shaman's chanting was opening the way into the spirit world where she knew her mate awaited them because she felt his presence. She was also aware of the other spirits involved in this journey. Her brother, White Bull was there, as was their shaman, Many Moons. She sensed another Cheyenne mystic, Charlie Littlebear who was linked with her husband's spirit. They were all coming together in the Spirit World, the place where all spirits passed on journeys to and from the various levels of space and time in the Great Spirit's realm. Their calling to Bryan would be successful, she knew, because both parties to the event were attuned to make this happen. Many Moons had assured her that their message was strong and good and the Great Spirit would grant their wishes.

Soon, she could see Bryan and Charlie Littlebear in the distance, their outlines dim, but recognizable. Their figures became clearer and began to draw nearer, an aura around them growing brighter and brighter until the light filled her senses and her point of focus was her man's figure.

Bryan was dressed in the clothing she had made for him, bore on his arm the shield that White Bull had helped him make, and he carried the heavy-hafted spear he had made. In his belt was the copper blade, a gift from Many Moons. Her heart filled with love and joy as his smiling face came closer and closer.

"Spirit Warrior," Many Moons voice was heard in her mind, "come with us back to your place in our lodges. The People need your skills, your wife is with child and needs you in the center of your lodge, and your brothers need your leadership. Your destiny is with your clan."

White Bull's voice was added to the call, "Bry-Yan, my brother, come back with us to your place with The People. We need you."

Her own voice was heard, "My husband. Our child grows within my belly, and my life is incomplete without you. Come back to me and your people."

"I am coming to you," came Bry-Yan's voice in her mind. The Great Spirit has sanctioned my journey to you." Without seeming to move, Bryan was at her side. She could feel his touch though his body hadn't moved. His love filled her heart and mind with ecstasy, and all of her needs were fulfilled.

Their mission and journey were nearly complete. Many Moons spirit spoke with Charlie Littlebear, "My brother, we thank you for your assistance to our Spirit Warrior. I sense that we will continue our contact with your spirit when we enter the spirit world from our respective doorways. Our relationship will be long and fruitful."

"Wise One, I am joyful that you, my ancestor, will be present to guide me on the pathway of The People. My spirit is renewed and will benefit The People of my time from this," said Charlie. Though his voice was in her mind, Strong Woman could sense the emotion.

Gradually, Charlie Littlebear's figure began to recede and grow dim, fading into the distance until he was gone. Bryan, her man, stayed at her side. She became aware of the ground underneath her, the discomfort in her legs from sitting during her spirit's long journey into the Spirit World, but she also felt the presence of her husband at her side. She turned her head and was again filled with joy at his smiling countenance. She fell into his arms and felt them tighten lovingly around her. The world was complete again.

THE COMING EVENT

His hand sleepily explored the distended stomach of his woman curled up against him. He could feel the baby pressing against his hand through her stomach. The child was very active at this early hour of the morning. Strong Woman moved a little under his ministrations, her sleep disturbed more by the movement of the baby in her womb than by her husband's gentle hand.

Bryan himself was only partly awake, roused slightly from a pleasant dream. He and Strong Woman were bundled in buffalo robes on a soft pallet in their lodge among The People. There were still some coals from the night fire glowing in the fire pit in the center of the lodge. Bryan stuck his arm out of the warmth of the soft robes and tossed a couple of small sticks on the coals, hoping to warm the teepee before he had to rise.

It was the dead of winter. The People had retired to their wintering grounds almost three months ago. They were in a protected valley near a year-round stream, but still, the winter had brought much snow and cold. It would be another month before the weather began to break allowing more than subsistence activity. The People spent much of their time repairing tools, weapons, and clothing during the quiet winter months. Some men braved the weather and hunted for game. Though their larders were well stocked with pemmican, dried meat—buffalo, elk, antelope, and deer—dried herbs, wild vegetables, plus the dried corn and other items they had traded for with the Pawnees, they felt the need for activity. The occasional fresh meat was a welcome respite from their normal winter fare.

The men of Bryan's karate training group had erected a large shelter for their continued workouts. Unlike the normal conical lodge of The People, this was a long, dome-shaped structure of curved stays of young, limber saplings, joined overhead and covered with buffalo hides. Several panels had been installed at regular intervals along the curve of the walls. These were of buffalo hides scraped so thin they were translucent, allowing diffused light to enter the structure. Bryan thought it looked like a buffalo skin Quonset hut, the type of building he had seen lots of during his US Army service. A fire pit at each end provided warmth and added light during their frequent karate training sessions. The building served also as a communal meeting place, a central place for social activity during the winter months and a storage place for firewood, bags of buffalo chips and other tinder for cook fires.

Several of the men had become very advanced students of Bryan's Go-ju Kempo system of karate. White Bull in particular was very adept and assisted his sensei in the training, leading the classes in the warm-ups, basic techniques, and beginning kata or forms. Five of the other warriors were advanced enough to have been awarded brown belts if they were in a modern karate dojo or school. This cadre formed the nucleus of what had become a warrior society, much like the Running Dog Lodge of Bryan's chief rival, Many Coups. The karate-ka had taken to calling themselves the Mountain Cat Lodge, harkening to the deadly skills of the puma, the big cat of North America.

Resigned to the lack of immediate heat from the tiny fire, Bryan crept carefully out of their bower so as not to awaken his love. He gathered a few more sticks and placed them on the small blaze, feeling some comfort in the immediate flare-up. After adding several small logs, he hurriedly dressed in his deerskins and moccasins, pulled on a buffalo hide coat, and went out to relieve himself. The predawn air was crisp and cold. There was stirring from the nearby lodges as fires were built up and water was being heated for cooking and bathing.

In his time among The People, Bryan had learned that personal hygiene was a general practice, involving frequent bathing, steam baths, teeth cleaning, and grooming. A proud and regal race, the Cheyenne kept their bodies very clean as well as their homes and attire. Their children were disciplined gently by any adults in the clan group as the members all acted and felt like an extended family, which indeed they were. All the men were "uncles" and the women were "aunts" of all the children. It was common practice for all of the adults to pass on their particular skills to any and all of the children in formal and informal sessions. The men taught hunting, fishing, and martial skills, while the women taught cooking, tanning, lodge tending, and other domestic skills.

The children could learn anything that interested them; thus, there were often girls involved in basic warrior training, and some of the boys learned homemaking skills as well. There was wide acceptance of any role the children chose to play, only an encouragement to do well in any chosen endeavor, because it would benefit the entire clan group.

His toilette finished, Bryan returned to the lodge, now warmed by the small blaze in the fire pit. Strong Woman had risen and dressed and was ready to leave the lodge to fill water bladders from the nearby creek. Bryan took the bladders from her, urging her to sit while he fetched the water. Strong Woman still had some trouble to accepting her husband's assistance with what was normally "woman's work," but she knew it pleased him to help her, particularly since her pregnancy was so far advanced. As she did every morning, she thanked the Great Spirit for her man and asked for his continued health and well-being.

Like most Native Americans, the Plains peoples in particular, the Cheyenne were very spiritual. It was their belief that there was one Great Spirit who ruled over everything, but they also believed that all animate and inanimate objects possessed spirits and could either be friendly or adversarial to The People.

Later, after dining on a gruel of rehydrated pemmican with dried herbs and vegetables, Bryan left his lodge and made his way along the broad pathway in the snow to the lodge of White Bull, his best friend and brother-in-law. White Bull was waiting and arose from his pallet beside the fire when Bryan entered.

"You ready?" Bryan queried.

"Yes, of course," replied White Bull. "Anything to get my blood flowing in this cold."

They left the lodge and headed for the communal great lodge. They could see several other young men heading that way as well. It was time for their early karate training session. Once inside the big lodge, after the fires at each end had been stoked and fueled, Bryan and White Bull removed their outer garments and began their stretching exercises designed to loosen their joints and warm their muscles. By the time they were warmed up, they had been joined by two dozen other men and several younger boys and a few girls who were wearing leggings and shirts instead of dresses. The fires were blazing at either end of the great lodge, but it was still chilly on the training floor in the middle.

White Bull, as sempai, the senior student, called the class to order. They lined up in three rows, arranging themselves by level of skills, the most experienced students in the front row, intermediates in the middle, and the beginners in the rear.

On White Bull's command, the class faced Bryan and bowed, and he bowed in return. Another command from White Bull and the class assumed the horse-riding stance, left arm extended with the fist clenched and the right fist clenched at the hip. At a grunted command from the sempai, the class punched with their right hand while drawing the left back against their left hip. Another command and the left fist shot forward explosively. In this manner, alternating the punches, they completed fifty moves. Then they moved to double punches, striking twice at each command.

The next routine was high or rising blocks. From the last punching position, with the left fist and arm extended, right fist at the hip, the command was given, and the right forearm was snapped up to above the forehead, the arm forming an L shape, palm of the fist outward. The left fist had simultaneously arrived back at the hip. This was reversed on the next command, and in this manner, fifty rising blocks were completed. The warm-up continued through inside blocks, outside blocks, knife-hand blocks, all while the students remaining in place in the horse stance.

Next came kicking technique practice. The students rose from the horse stance and stood with their feet apart and both arms thrust stiffly down in front, fists clenched, the formal stance. On the command, they raised their right knee high, foot pointed at the floor directly under their knee. On the second command, the foot was thrust forward, leading with the ball of the foot, toes curled back...the ball of the foot being the intended striking area. On the third command, the knee was drawn up again with the foot underneath. On the fourth command, the right foot was lowered to the floor. The whole four-step move was accomplished while the students balanced on their left feet. What followed next was the same move with the left foot, then right again until fifty kicks had been completed. As with the punches, each kick was accompanied by a *kiai*, an explosion of sound.

On the next command, the entire kick was made in one motion—knee up, foot pointed, snapped forward sharply, returned to knee up, then placed on the floor. Fifty more kicks were completed. Bryan moved among the students correcting their techniques, stances and favoring a few with compliments.

More kicks followed using the same approach—first making each of the four moves on command, next completing the whole kick in one move. Side kicks, roundhouse kicks, turning-back kicks, axe kicks, crescent kicks.

About sixty minutes had passed to this point. After a brief breather, the class was called to attention again, this time assuming the formal stance—feet apart, arms stiffly thrust downwards in front, fists clenched. White Bull gave the command.

"Moving forward, left foot first...down block!"

The students stepped forward with their left foot, and at the same time, they raised their left fist to their right cheek and extended their right arm stiffly down in front. As their left foot hit the ground, the left fist and arm were brought sharply down to a point above their left knee, and their right fist was chambered at the hip. Their finishing stance was stretched out, left leg forming an L, right leg stretched nearly straight behind, body erect in the middle, left fist over left knee, right fist chambered. A shouted *kiai* accompanied each move.

On the next command, the class stepped forward with their right feet, staying in the low position and performing the down block with the right arm and fist. By the end of the third move, they had reached the end of the great lodge. On the next command, they moved the trailing left leg and foot to the left, then swiveled their body around while performing another down block. In this manner, they moved up and down the training floor three more times.

Next came more moving blocks—inside, outside, rising, and finally the knife-hand blocks, this latter from a back stance, left leg forward with foot pointed ahead, weight over the right leg, hands formed in a knife edge with the left hand high by the right ear, the right hand thrust down across the body near the left hip. On the command, the left hand was snapped forward with the right drawn to the lower chest, palm up. On the next command, they shifted their weight to the left leg, stepped forward with the right, while bringing the right knife hand to the left ear, the left palm down at the right hip, snapping the right hand forward as the foot came down.

After about two hours, the basic technique training was over, and Bryan assumed command of the class with White Bull taking up the number one position in the first line of students. He explained that he was going to teach them a new kata, Teki-Sho, the first of three kata that emulated fighting off attackers while backed against a wall. He demonstrated the kata—the exaggerated lateral moves, blocking, parrying, thrusting, stepping high over fallen opponents—as he moved first to his left, then to his right, then returning to the center, and finishing in a powerful horse-riding stance. He rose erect and bowed. Then he broke the kata down into individual moves, explaining what each move translated to. Finally, he had the class perform the individual moves, moving among them, correcting any flaws in stance or technique.

After about half an hour, he led the class slowly through the kata. Most of them had a basic grasp of the moves, and soon, they were performing the form at half speed. He broke the class into small groups, each led by a more accomplished student, and had them practice the moves until all had some degree of expertise.

Bryan closed the practice session with one-step sparring. He paired the students—one being an attacker, the other a defender. The beginning move was a straight punch while the defender used a rising block. They switched roles, then switched to a front kick and down-block parry, and so on through a dozen or more attacks and blocks.

The students were formed into ranks again by White Bull's command. Bryan stood in front, and they all bowed to him and he bowed back.

"Tomorrow," said the sensei, "we will go through all our kata, then freestyle sparring, kumite."

The class broke for the day. White Bull and Bryan remained behind to bank the fires and talk a bit.

"Spring will be coming soon," said Bryan. "Then we must travel to meet with the professor and work out our plan. You will come with me, but probably I will leave Strong Woman here. I want her near her mother when her time comes."

THE PLAN

Charles Branson, the professor, lived among the Skidi, Wolf Pawnee, where he had been deposited by his trip through the Spirit World about a year earlier than Bryan had made his spectral trip. After he and Bryan met, they both calculated that if there were two of them, there were probably more others among other Indian tribes across the country. That they had been drawn through the Spirit World for some purpose was a known fact, but the *why* was a puzzle. Branson figured that there was an overall purpose, the answer to which lay in the skills they had developed in their former lives that there was need of in this time and place.

Branson had been a professor at Texas Agricultural and Mechanical University in College Station, Texas, USA, where he taught range science and agronomy. After arriving amongst the Pawnee, who lived in permanent villages and practiced a rudimentary agriculture, the professor set about to improve their crops by introducing irrigation, crop rotation, harvesting, and preserving techniques. It had been working well, and the Pawnee had bumper crops in their last two growing seasons.

Bryan and the professor had discussed a plan to locate other Spirit World travelers, learn what skills they brought with them, then organize lines of communications between them all. It was the professor's idea that when the coming winter passed into spring, several parties should be sent out to explore and locate any travelers. A meeting would be planned for all travelers and representatives of their host tribes, the location of which should be in some central point. The professor seemed to recall that in pre-Columbian times, there was a permanent Indian City at Cahokia, near the convolution of the Mississippi, Illinois, and Missouri Rivers. As the scholar recalled from his reading, Cahokia, at one time, had a population of more than twenty thousand people, making it larger than either London or Paris of the late-fourteenth century. Branson was unsure at exactly what stage of development or decline Cahokia was in. His astronomical estimates had no accurate benchmark, but he had calculated from his knowledge of the heavens that the present time was somewhere in the mid 1300s, probably about 150 years before European exploration of the Western Hemisphere, maybe even earlier than that.

Charles Branson had the entire winter to ponder their situation. He and Bryan figured that they were not the only ones to have made the trip through the Spirit World to a pre-Columbian era in North America. All they knew for sure was that they each came from approximately the same time period, around the turning of the twentieth into the twenty-first century. If there were more others, did they come from the same era, or some other era where their technology was just developing and more appropriate to application to the world in which Bryan and the professor found themselves?

The professor couldn't be sure if he had really traveled back in time or was he in a parallel world? The more he pondered this the more he was convinced that since the transfer had been immediate, the spirit world was a portal between parallel time periods. He further surmised that what Bryan and he achieved, and the actions of any others drawn here, it would be reflected in either world. In either case, he believed that it was his role, and that of any others, to change the future of the American Indians and thus the past in his own time. He had convinced himself that it was his mission to bring technical advances in agronomy to the Indians, just as Bryan was to teach martial arts as a route to peace between the tribes, as much as it was to strengthen the Cheyenne people. What other types of technology would be represented by other Spirit World travelers? They had to find out.

The mechanics of both Bryan and his arrival in this world also captured some of the professor's meditations. Both of them had been sleeping, or hypnotized in Bryan's case, but that is a state of total relaxation like sleep. Thus they were vulnerable to the call from beyond the spirit world. Their specific selection brought skills they could contribute to the betterment of this time and place, thus, he speculated, any others similarly transported would have skills of importance.

During the wintering period, the professor's hosts, the Skidi Pawnee, had come through without any suffering. The food stores were greatly augmented by the bumper harvest created by the farming methods taught by Branson, and further enlarged by trading preserved corn, edible gourds, and other produce with neighboring tribes for parfleches of pemmican, dried meats, and fish.

THE PLAN FOR
SEEKING THE OTHERS

The weather broke, and the days became warmer. Much of the snow had melted, except for drifts on the north side of hillocks and in ravines. The spring flooding from the runoff of the snow melt was abating. Bryan was restless and became impatient to travel to the Skidi Pawnee village to meet with the professor and plan how they were going to make contact with the others who came through the Spirit World to this time and place.

It was decided that Bryan and White Bull would leave on the morrow, and they packed the clothing and other items they would need for the journey of an anticipated four or five days, barring any natural barriers or unforeseen difficulties. Strong Woman was nearing her time and would stay in the village of The People in case their child arrived early.

The two men departed before first light and were miles along the way when the sun rose and began to warm the day. They were proceeding at a fast dogtrot, a pace they could keep up for many hours. Instead of stopping to eat, they chewed jerky which nourished and staved off hunger until they would stop for the night and would eat a more fulfilling meal.

They made very good time the first day and paused to rest near a small, swift creek that was still slightly swollen from the spring thaw. Shortly before they stopped, Bryan's throwing stick brought down a prairie chicken that flushed from a thatch of buffalo grass almost at their feet. In their temporary camp, Bryan cleaned the bird while White Bull made a small cooking fire from hastily gathered dead branches. With the bird spitted and cooking, the men gathered more dead wood from under the trees lining the creek bank and stacked it close at hand to their campfire.

To supplement the cooked bird, Bryan had cleaned some tree bark that was formed into a natural bowl. He put water from the stream into this and placed this cooking pot on a mesh of green branches above the fire, making sure that the fire was lower than the water level in the improvised bowl. When the water was boiling, he shaved pieces of pemmican into the bark pot from a small block in his pack. Soon, there was a savory stew to accompany the bird.

After their meal, the two men rolled into their traveling robes alongside the fire. During the night, one of them awakened and fed more fuel to their small blaze. Before first light, they were both up and packed up their robes. After a quick toilette, they were again on the trail. They had forded the cold stream the evening before while holding their clothes and packs overhead. Now, they quickly dressed and headed northwest, their running quickly warming their bodies that had been chilled somewhat by the night spent under the light robes.

Three days after they left, they camped for the last night about half a day's journey from the Skidi Pawnee village. On the morrow, they would be in the professor's lodge, making their plans.

It was in midmorning when they topped a small rise and looked down into the Pawnee village of permanent wood-sided and roofed lodges. Scouts had known of their coming for several hours, and the professor and the Pawnee leaders were waiting for them. They greeted each other warmly with masculine hugs and backslapping. They entered the lodge and seated themselves around the fire. After the pipe-smoke ritual and necessary small talk was exchanged, the professor got right to the point.

"I have had all winter to plan, as I am sure you have too. I strongly believe that we will find people of assorted skills amongst other tribes around the country, and we should have everyone come together at some central point so we can assess what we are able to do to form some sort of organization of tribes." The professor went on, "If my thoughts are correct, we are here in this time to utilize all the talents we brought to enrich the lives of these native peoples and bring them together with the common goal of trading alliances and a peaceful coexistence."

It was decided that three-man teams would be sent from both the Pawnee and Cheyenne villages. Initial contacts would be made on other clan groups and villages from these two tribes and then expanded in an ever-increasing circle to the other neighboring tribes. If any other spirit world travelers were found, a runner would be sent back to the Skidi Pawnee village of the professor, who was to coordinate the efforts to have a centrally located meeting of all the others. Everyone agreed with the professor's idea of forming a coalition of all these skilled people to share their technology with all the Indian tribes who came into the confederation they wanted to form.

The time for implementing their plan was close. Bryan and White Bull had solicited volunteers from the Mountain Cat Society, and a meeting was held with Faces West, the chief, and Many Moons, the shaman. The messengers were to be paired up and given sacred belts of shells, wampum, as an indication of their peaceful intentions. It was decided to send the first men toward the east and southeast because the more populous tribes lived in those directions. The plan was simple, locate any more others who had passed through the Spirit World, tell them about Bryan and the professor, and learn what special skills they possessed. Also they wanted to inform the tribal leaders of the future threat that colonization efforts from Europe presented to all the Americas. The professor had also put together a group of volunteers from the Skidi and Cahuai Pawnee. The initial plan was to solicit more volunteer runners from the tribes they contacted, thus multiplying their efforts exponentially with every contact.

THE MISSION BEGINS

Bryan had decided to await the arrival of his child rather than head up a team of runners to other tribes. He wanted to be on hand for the birth of his child and help Strong Woman in any way he could though he knew that her mother would probably shoo him out of the birthing lodge when the time came. Most men of The People did little to assist in such female matters though they did stay nearby to lend moral support. During the delay in his participation in the search for more spirit travelers, Bryan would receive reports from the runner teams and forward information to the professor for compilation.

Bryan gathered the volunteers from their Mountain Cat Lodge and a number of others from Many Coup's Running Dog Lodge who had joined the mission despite the tacit resistance from their lodge leader. It had been planned that three warriors would be on each team of runners. After they had reached another village and met with the elders to explain their mission, they would then seek more volunteers to join with the original team, two new members with each original runner. In this manner, after each stop three new teams would set out. Runners would be sent back to the Cheyenne and Pawnee villages with information about any other travelers. The professor had estimated that they could cover at least one quarter of the USA portion of North America before late autumn.

It was the initial goal to compile a list of all the spirit world travelers and the skills they possessed. After which, they would convene a meeting at a central location, somewhere on the upper Mississippi River, maybe at the legendary Indian city of Cahokia just north of present day St. Louis, if it existed in this time and place. In Bryan and the professor's time, it was known that Cahokia had been a city of between fifteen and twenty thousand residents at some point between the sixth and the fifteenth centuries, making it larger than either Paris or Rome of that time. Little is known of the people who built the city or why it ultimately disappeared. It was apparently an intertribal trading center with permanent wooden houses and a thriving populace.

White Bull was given a choice of assignments and opted to take his team northeast in the direction of several other Cheyenne clan groups and, ultimately, the lands of the Dakota people. At the last moment, Many Coups swallowed his pride and offered to lead a group, there was no way he was going to miss out on this adventure, warrior that he was. His decision was well received by Bryan, White Bull, and the other volunteers.

EXECUTION OF THE PLAN

The professor and Bryan had spent a lot of time composing a plan they taught to all the teams that had volunteered to carry it out. Everyone knew their mission was to find out how many more Spirit World travelers there were, where they were located, and what special skills they brought with them. The plan was not complex, just the gathering of information, so the professor and Bryan could make a more accurate guess as to the reason for all the travelers and then plan the next steps to accomplish the tasks intended for them. The special skills listing would go a long way toward their understanding of their purpose.

All the spirit world travelers they found would be invited to meet in a central location, the Indian city of Cahokia near the convolution of the Mississippi and Illinois Rivers, about thirty miles north of present-day St. Louis. This meeting would take place the following year in the late spring.

Most of the Plains Indians had done a lot of traveling in their hunter-gatherer lifestyle, and many of them had intercourse with other tribes, some even learning rudimentary language skills. All of them were conversant in the sign language common to all the tribes. Selection of the initial destinations for the teams was based upon who was familiar with which nearby tribes.

White Bull and his team were heading northeast to the lands of the Dakotas. Many Coups was taking his team southwest toward the southern plains, the lands of the Arapaho and Comanche. Most of teams from the Pawnee villages were heading north and west and were expected to come in contact with the Crow, Blackfoot, Flathead, and other northern plains tribes. After his child was born, Bryan intended to head east with several more teams, the intent being to split up after they crossed the Mississippi River and locating Cahokia, if it was there at all.

THE SMITHY

"Under the spreading chestnut tree, the village smithy stands."

The opening line from that old poem ran through his mind while he worked in his backyard forge. Earlier, the smith had removed the bloom from the furnace, then eliminated a lot of the impurities by repeated working of the raw metal at low heat until he had a ball of hot iron that was ready for forging.

With his tongs, he held the iron on the anvil and beat it gently as possible, forming an iron bar that would later be forged into implements, axes, knife blades, spear points, and arrowheads. The neighbor boy who often helped him, was working the bellows to keep the charcoal fire at the right temperature for frequent immersions of the iron being worked, a process that removed the remnants of slag and carbon, leaving nearly pure iron.

Larry Stamps was a big, broad-framed man with large, thick-fingered hands, sturdy wrists, and powerful forearms and biceps. By trade, he was a mechanical engineer, but his hobby was making iron tools in his backyard forge. Often from iron, he smelted himself in his bloomery, a furnace for making small quantities of good-quality iron. He hadn't yet graduated to making steel, but he was familiar with the Bessemer process whereby steel was created from raw iron.

Big Larry was a production manager for a kitchen appliance manufacturer near Dayton, Ohio. He lived alone, having not found the right woman to share his life. He had lots of friends, several of which were women who might be prospective mates. He had a moderately active social life, much of which was with those who shared his interests.

Larry had a number of hobbies, one of which was to use primitive methods to smelt iron. Others of his hobbies included physical challenges like working out with prodigious weights, wilderness orienteering, hunting with primitive weapons and camping in remote areas using little or no modern conveniences. He was really drawn to physical challenges.

Larry attributed his hobby interests to his mechanical engineering education, for the iron smelting, and his love of physical challenges and the great outdoors. The latter interest, the big man felt could be genetic, as according to passed down family lore, several of his ancestors were Shawnee Indians.

His life was orderly (the trait of an engineer) and his financial success was more than moderate, but Larry wasn't entirely satisfied with his existence. He felt that there was more to life than running a manufacturing operation and his hobbies. *Maybe it's my single status?* he thought. *But I don't want to marry unless it is definitely the right person for me.*

For a number of months, Big Larry's normally peaceful sleep had been interrupted by dreams in which he felt himself drawn through a misty portal to an unknown destination. At first he passed this off as indigestion or an anomaly caused by his vivid imagination as influenced by television movies or the books he was always reading. Lately, though, the dreams had become more intense and he could sense the presence of another person or persons beyond the mist.

All that ended one morning in early spring when he awakened and found himself lying naked in a forest glade on the shores of a great body of water. For several weeks prior to this event, Big Larry's strange, nightly dreams took the form of a summons as if from a great distance, someone or something was calling to him, but he didn't know who or why.

Larry was resourceful if nothing else, so when he found himself in a strange place, he set about to learn where he was and why. For some reason, he didn't question that he was involved in a mystical event. Probably because of his engineer's practicality, he just accepted the fact that either he was having a very realistic and very long dream, or he had been transported to another place and time by some means not understood.

A short hike along the shore of the lake had brought him to an Indian village nestled in a clearing. The dwellings were bark covered semicircular frames numbering about a dozen. They were similar to what he remembered reading about the longhouses of the Eastern

Woodlands tribes, usually built to house an extended family or several families.

From concealment on the forested shore, he scanned the village. There were a few people moving among the lodges, mostly children, while in the adjacent field, women were at work in what appeared to be rows of corn, the plants in low hills were about a foot tall and were in orderly rows. There were a few men in evidence, mostly elders in a couple of small groups, and it was on one of these his gaze fell. An older man was seated in front of one of the lodges, leaning against a backrest frame. Seated across from him where two other men both appearing past their prime but not as much as the ancient one. They were all dressed in buckskin shirts, leggings, breech cloths, and moccasins, but the elder had on what appeared to be a shell gorget stretched across his upper chest. Big Larry had a feeling that this old man might be the cause of his being in this place.

He figured that these people would not feel threatened by a naked man, so throwing caution to the winds, he rose and left his concealment and began walking toward the old man and his companions. He was noticed immediately by the trio and several of the women. The old man arose and moved a few steps toward the oncoming naked stranger.

Big Larry raised both hands, holding them palms outward to show they were empty, and the old man responded by holding out his right palm and uttering a few words in an unintelligible tongue and what Larry presumed to be a greeting. The old man did not appear to be surprised at the arrival of this big, naked stranger.

In the succeeding six months, Big Larry learned that he was among the People of the Lake, as this clan group of Ojibwa was known by their neighbors. He had been taught the universal sign language of North American Indians and was well on his way to an expanded vocabulary in the Algonquin-based language of the Lake People.

The old man, the village shaman, called He Who Sees Far for his mystical connection with the Spirit World, could only tell Big Larry that he was here for a reason, but he could not tell what reason. He did say that he had been called through the Spirit World to perform some task that would be disclosed to Big Larry by the spirits or Great Spirit when the time was right.

Larry had put aside disquieting thoughts and began to adapt to life with the Lake People who lived in harmony with their natural surroundings—planting, hunting, and fishing. Their primary crops were corn, squash, and beans. Their primary quarry was deer and elk with an occasional foray onto the plains for buffalo. The great lake was teemed with fish—salmon, trout, and pike. Much of their time was spent gathering and processing food for the winter season. The men did the hunting and fishing, and the women tended the vegetable crops, made clothing and did much of the cooking. Both of them raised and trained the children.

During one of his exploration forays into the surrounding low hills, Larry noticed an outcropping of rock jutting from the side of a low cliff. The rock was stained with red streaks indicative of a ferrous ore vein. An idea was born.

Enlisting the assistance of several of the teenaged young men, the big man dug a copious amount of clay from a stream bank, clay that the women normally used to make pottery bowls and implements. With the clay, he formed a cylindrical chamber about five feet tall, open at both ends with a small hole about two feet up from the base and a larger opening cut out at the bottom. He fired the clay by building a hardwood fire in the center and keeping it going for a couple of days. He stabilized the outside by wrapping it in wet rawhide, which, when dried, provided a hard shell. It was crude, but he had fashioned a bloomery in which to smelt the iron ore.

With the continued assistance of the young men, Big Larry erected an open-sided shelter as his forge and made a bed of sand for the bloomery. Making hardwood charcoal was the next task.

They assembled a huge stack of five-foot long logs and arranged them vertically like a tent. Leaving an air hole at the bottom, they plastered the exterior with clay, then lit a fire in the center. The fire drew the moisture from the wood and, after a time, began to turn the logs dark brown, then brown-black. At this point, the logs were about 90 percent carbon and right for firing the bloomery. Big Larry and his helpers broke the dry, brittle charcoal logs into small, walnut-sized chunks, better for feeding the bloomery.

Larry fashioned a tuyere (pronounced twee-er) from clay and fired it. The tuyere is a tube that feeds air into the bloomery and is installed in the side at a downwards angle of about twenty degrees. To feed the air, a primitive bellows was made using wood and leather. The same bellows would be used later in the forge.

The iron ore was gathered and roasted in an open fire to drive off water. Now they were ready to make iron.

For the smelting, equal parts of charcoal and iron ore were stacked into the bloomery. The charcoal was then ignited. The helpers, spelling each other every half hour or so, kept pressurized air flowing into the stack by pumping the bellows steadily. As the mixture lowered in the flue, equal parts of ore and charcoal were added until they had used up about seventy-five pounds of each. After this last addition of the ore-charcoal mix, when the level of material in the bloomery lowered enough, another ten pounds of charcoal was added to the top. The stack was allowed to burn down to the tuyere level, the bellows pumping was halted, the tube was removed, and the hole plugged with a wet wood stopper.

After the charcoal had burned out and the bloomery cooled somewhat, it was tipped on its side and a bloom of raw iron removed from where it had formed against the side of the ceramic wall. The bloom weighed about twenty-five pounds but still contained some of the charcoal and slag. This would be removed in the forging process.

The first items Larry made from his iron were an anvil and blacksmithing tools. He was now on his fourth batch of iron and had begun to fashion knife blades and tomahawk heads. He took the first of his efforts to

Sees Far, a nicely forged knife with a blade about nine inches long and a six-inch tang that he had wrapped in a rawhide strip for a handle and a tomahawk head with a sharp blade on one side, a spike on the other, a sleeve for the wood shaft in the middle. The old shaman was very pleased and impressed with the iron tools.

Big Larry then set about making several large iron cooking pots and assorted smaller ones. He became very popular with the women of the tribe. He was now in the process of making another batch of spear points, arrowheads, tomahawk, and axe heads. All the men of the Lake People had these implements, but this next batch was for trading with other Ojibwa clans.

His personal life was looking up as well. A number of young women had shown interest in the big, broad-faced, smiling man. His language skills had progressed so that he was conversant enough to carry on a rudimentary conversation. Sees Far and a couple of the elders had been mentoring Big Larry, counseling him on the mores and folkways of the Ojibwa, as well as teaching him their tongue. Sees Far, with subtle humor, had pointed out to Larry, the interest of the young women.

"The other men want you to pick one, so all of the marriageable women aren't mooning over you while ignoring them," said the old shaman. Big Larry was a little flustered and didn't quite know how to react. Sees Far went on, "You need a good woman to care for your needs. There are several who would be good choices, so take a little time away from your work and get to know them."

THE HORSEMAN

The Bar T was a real working ranch. Located in the Texas Hill Country about one hundred miles west of Austin, the terrain was rolling and oak covered with large open pastures and a number of streams. Encompassing about a quarter of a million acres, the Bar T wasn't a particularly large ranch by Texas standards, but it was well staffed and tended. They were known for the quality of the horses they raised, as well as their beef herd.

Steve Ross was the foreman of the horse operation. A compact, muscular man of medium height, he moved with an easy grace that belied his muscularity. Accompanied by several other hands, Steve was moving a large herd of quarter horses to holding pens near the main ranch in preparation for their annual auction sale, a big event at the Bar T. The herd was a mixture of mares with foals and recently bred fillies, also a couple dozen stallions, about five hundred head total. Stallions were usually kept separate and seldom offered for sale in the auctions, but this herd was made up of several breeding groups that had been gathered for the short drive to the sale. The studs would be separated from the herd at the pens.

He was very much "into" horses, and had been so all of his life. He was raised on a small West Texas ranch and had been riding almost since he had learned to walk. He had worked for horse breeders and ranchers since becoming an adult and his knowledge and understanding of horses, was widely known in equine circles. This was why the owner of the Bar T had sought him out and hired him to run the horse breeding operation. Steve loved life on the ranch, but he wished that he could have lived when horses were very important to daily life and not just an anomaly from the past.

This area of the Bar T was fenced and cross fenced into pastures of several hundred to several thousand acres each, with large double gates on each side. The point riders in the drive preceded the herd and opened the gates then passed through with the herd following. The drag drivers trailing the herd closed the gates after the last horse passed through. There were roads on the ranch, but the size of the horse herd dictated the crossing of the pastures instead of squeezing the herd down into a road-sized string.

These broodmares had been in several of the far pastures, nearly twenty miles from the holding pens. Because of the number of foals and not wanting to bring them in worn out, the cowboys were making an overnight trip of the drive. They were about five miles from the ranch headquarters when they bedded the herd for the night in a large-fenced pasture. Most of the cowhands settled down around the cook fire by the chuckwagon that had been waiting for them, while two of their number circled around the herd on horseback until the mares were grazing and nursing foals. Later at night, they would post only one night rider to keep the animals quiet.

It was dusk when Steve rode into the camp circle. He could smell the handiwork of the cook as he tied his horse with the others on the ramuda line stretched between two trees. There were large beefsteaks grilling over a mesquite fire with a huge coffeepot and equally large pot of beans bubbling alongside. The aroma of biscuits in the dutch oven added to the intoxicating smells of the food. The cook was laying out bowls of vegetables on the table that dropped down from the side of the wagon. There would be a fruit cobbler for dessert. The Bar T fed their hardworking hands well.

Steve stripped the saddle from his horse and carried it into the circle where he would use it for a seat for dinner, then a pillow at night. Most of the other hands had already retrieved their bedrolls from the chuckwagon and were seated, nursing cups of coffee, awaiting the cook's call to dinner. He got his bedroll and laid it on the saddle to soften his seat for dinner, his butt being tired enough from a day in this same saddle.

After dinner, coffee and conversation ensued for an hour or so, but gradually, the cowhands began to turn in. They would be up before dawn for biscuits and coffee and then continue the drive. Steve stripped to his shorts and crawled into his bedroll, using his folded jeans and shirt as a cushion on the saddle. His boots and hat were close at hand. Though he was the boss, Steve shared the night work with his hands and intended to take the last night rider shift before dawn. He had broken the task into two hour shifts, so no one would lose much sleep.

It seemed like he had hardly closes his eyes when he was shaken awake by the ranch hand who had the previous watch. Harry Tyler, a tall lanky galoot, loomed above him, his dark shape lit by the few flickering logs left from the cook fire. Steve had been in the midst of a very realistic, but strange dream, one in which he was herding the horses toward a shimmering opening in the trees, and he awoke with a start.

"Rise and shine, Segundo," said the cowboy. "Things are quiet. There were a couple of coyotes sniffing around the foals, but that big red stud ran them off."

Steve rolled out of his bedroll and slipped into his jeans and boots, then shrugged into his shirt. He rolled his bedding and carried it to the chuckwagon where he stowed it away. Grabbing his saddle by the horn, he headed to the ramuda, the line of horses tied to a rope strung between two trees. He saddled and bridled his mount, swung into the saddle and headed toward the pasture where the horse herd was bedded. The camp was quiet. The cook would awaken soon and begin preparing the breakfast of biscuits, bacon, and strong coffee.

He swung the wide gate open without dismounting and then closed it behind him as his horse moved into the pasture. In the dim starlight, he could see the dark shapes of the horses loosely bunched near the far end, near some trees lining the creek that cut through the enclosure. His saddle creaked under his shifting weight as he walked his big bay gelding across the field. Still a little troubled by his dream, which he remembered in detail, he neared the horse herd and began to slowly circle the dozing equines, the slow clopping of his horse's pace not disturbing any of the animals.

As he circled the herd counter-clockwise toward the tree-lined creek, the full moon gave him good visibility. He noticed that some of the horses were raising their heads and looking in the direction of the creek. More and more of the animals roused and began to look in the same direction. A few who were closer to the creek began to move in that way, heads up, ears pricked and alert, as they slowly walked toward the trees together. More of the horses began to move that way until most of the herd was moving slowly toward the corner of the pasture and the creek.

Steve stood in his stirrups in an attempt to see further, but there was nothing visible, only the blackness of the shadows under creek willows. His horse, too, was alert and staring at the darkness; then, the gelding began to walk, following the herd. Steve gave him his head as he peered into the gloom, trying to see what was drawing the horses. Far ahead, the lead horses began to disappear down the bank to the creek, still moving at a walk.

The pace picked up a bit, and soon, the horses were moving at a trot toward the creek bank. As his horse, trailing the last of the herd, neared the creek, Steve could see that there was a deeper darkness at the point where the animals were going over the bank. As he peered, the darkness seemed to shimmer slightly, as if it were a physical thing. Ten abreast the horses were passing into the darkness and disappearing from view.

THE MEDICAL TEAM

Arthur Schwaninger, MD, was an immunologist specializing in developing vaccines to protect military personnel from tropical diseases, a host of which seemed to be popping up almost weekly. A lieutenant-colonel in the US Air Force, Art had been plying his trade for more than twenty years at various military hospitals and research facilities around the world. His current duty station was at Andrews AFB in the Washington, DC, area. His love was research, and he immersed himself into this field, body and soul; thus, he was probably at the acme of his career. Had he been more of a political animal, he would probably have a star on his shoulder before he retired, but that wasn't in the cards.

Mary, Art's wife, was a registered nurse, so she had no trouble transferring her career along with her husband's moves, nursing being a high-demand profession. Their children were grown and gone, so there was little disruption from transfers or temporary duty assignments.

A tall, fit, and handsome couple who looked like a judge and his wife or a senator and her husband, they favored outdoor pursuits in their limited off-duty time—camping, hunting, fishing, hiking, and biking. They were both adept outdoorsmen.

When Art began to have disturbing dreams about working hard to develop vaccines and inoculating a very large number of people, dreams that he remembered all the details after awakening, he shared this with Mary. To his surprise, she told him that she had also been having similar dreams. Their conclusion was that they were both working too hard and they should take some time off for a camping trip to one of their favorite areas on the Appalachian Trail in North Carolina. Art took two weeks' leave, and Mary took vacation time.

With growing excitement, Art and Mary packed for the trip, being sure to include a number of books for light reading, and nothing of a medical nature. They loaded up their diesel-powered SUV with their tent, sleeping bags, air mattresses, double mantle lanterns, cooking gear, and food supply and headed out. They left early in the morning, so they would be at the campgrounds before nightfall.

Arriving at the remote campgrounds in mid-afternoon, they pitched their tent, dug the rain run-off trench around the perimeter, pumped up their air mattresses, and laid out their sleeping bags. Art hung the lanterns from the tent center pole and then turned to setting up the cooking area.

They had brought a circular steel fire ring that Art placed over the fire pit he dug. He pounded a long, thick steel stake at the edge of the fire ring. The stake had a metal stop midway down that was where the cooking grate would rest, the grate being able to be rotated away from the fire so the cook didn't get singed while placing or removing food. After sliding the grate down over the stake, Art rotated it a few times to make sure he had driven the stake deeply enough to anchor the apparatus, so it wouldn't tilt after he had steaks on the grille. A steel framework was then opened up and placed next to the fire ring. This would be placed over one side of the ring for pots and pans.

Art really loved outdoor cooking, and Mary was very content to let him show off his skills. She sat nearby, leaning against her backrest, glass of wine in hand, and watched his preparations. He had told her the menu was grilled rib-eye steaks, his famous baked beans, steamed broccoli, and a nice garden salad accompanied by a good, dry red wine, of course.

Not counting on finding firewood for their first night in camp, Art had packed two large bags of charcoal briquettes. He dumped a double handful into his chimney-type charcoal lighter, crushed one piece of newspaper, placed that under the chimney, and lit it with a kitchen match. In about fifteen minutes, the coals were glowing white-hot. Art dumped this into the fire pit and added fresh briquettes around the sides and a thin layer over the top. In another half hour, the fire was a glowing pit of coals.

While the fire was getting ready, Art had taken the steaks, jars of already prepared beans, vegetables, and salad from the cooler. The beans were placed in a cast-iron pot and put on the metal frame that Art had settled on one side of the fire pit opposite the rotating grille. The broccoli was put in another pot that held the steamer cradle and an inch of water. He seasoned the vegetable with salt and pepper and placed the lid on the pot and put it next to the bean pot.

The salad fixings went into a large bowl. Art cut some tomatoes into the greens and tossed it all with a vinegar, oil, and garlic dressing. He served Mary and himself a bowl of salad that they contentedly munched while the beans were heating and the broccoli was steaming. Salad finished, Art rose and rotated the grille out over the hot coals. He then seasoned the steaks on both sides. In five minutes, the grille was hot and the steaks sizzled as he carefully placed them on the grille to cook.

The whole meal came together with perfect timing. They sat back and sighed contentedly when they had finished their medium rare steaks, delicious baked beans, steamed broccoli, and a couple of glasses of Cabernet. Art and Mary had always adhered to the principle that "roughing it" was not necessary to having a good time in a natural setting. They had spent years accumulating their camping gear and learning how to be comfortable in the great outdoors, and this trip showed that they learned their lessons well.

It had grown dark while they dined. Art had found a couple of large pine knots in the edge of the woods, and he threw these on the bed of coals. The pitch in the pine flared up, and their camp was well lighted. The warmth was welcome here in the high country, where most nights were cool.

After enjoying the campfire for a while, they rose as one and retired to their tent. Art had placed all the food leftovers in a container and put everything back in the cooler. He had thrown a rope over a tree limb at the edge of their camp, and with that, he pulled the cooler up to where bears and other critters couldn't reach and tied the rope off to the tree trunk. No food was left on the ground or in their vehicle.

Art lighted one of the lanterns and they both read for a while before rolling up in their sleeping bags. It was only minutes before Art's gentle snores were the only sound in camp.

A black bear sow and a couple of raccoon checked out the camp during the night, but the lack of available food made their visits short.

In the morning, Art and Mary awoke naked on the bare ground with all of their camping gear gone.

THE LINGUIST

Rosetta Herrera-Lozano had always had a fascination with and a flair for languages. Raised in a bilingual house with the Spanish of her Mexican-born father and the English of her California-raised mother, she probably had a head start on most children. Then an uncle visited from Mexico, her grandfather's brother, and she heard her first words in a Native American tongue. Her father's people were from the mountains of Northern Mexico, the Sierra Madre, and their lineage was liberally sprinkled with a mixture of Jicarilla Apache and the wild and fearsome Seri, the people of the mountains and desert around the Sea of Cortez.

Rose excelled in high school and was awarded an academic scholarship to the University of California–San Diego. Her major was Spanish, and when she did her graduate degree, it was in Indigenous Languages of North America.

An athletically built woman, Rose also enjoyed and excelled in field sports—field hockey, soccer, and track. Rose had strong rather than pretty features, but her soft eyes and wonderful smile made her beautiful. She was healthy, hearty, and loved all the history of the peoples who made up her heritage.

Faced with the problem of many academics, how to make a living after graduation with a PhD, Rose turned to teaching at her alma mater, University of San Diego. From this close-to-the-border location, Rose made frequent forays into Northern Mexico, the land of her forebearers. From these study trips, she learned more of the language of the Seri and Apache than she had from her great-uncle. She was also exposed to the other indigenous languages of Northern Mexico and Southwestern United States. Rose became an expert in the tongues of the western area of North America. She immersed herself in her studies and had little time for a personal life.

Rose had always felt that her life and interests were to serve some important purpose. She was frustrated that she hadn't yet found her niche, but somewhere in her future was the role she had been created to play in the scheme of things. She enjoyed teaching, but it was not fulfilling, this being the reason for her deep interest and energy spent in learning more about her heritage and the pursuit of greater knowledge of primitive American languages.

On one of her recent trips, Rose was in a small village in the mountains of Baja California near San Felipe, a commercial shrimping village on the Sea of Cortez. Here she encountered an ancient medicine man who asked to speak privately with her. She agreed and went to his shack, a hovel on the edge of the town, to meet.

The shack was dark with only a flickering light from several candles on shelves and one in the center of the rough-hewn table in the center of the room. The old man bade her be seated and spoke to her in the Seri language.

"I have a message from beyond the Spirit World," he began. "You will be traveling through the Spirit World sometime soon. Prepare yourself."

"What do you mean, the Spirit World?" asked Rose.

"All life, before, now, and the future is connected through the Spirit World," replied the old man. "Your destiny may be in your traveling. Follow your instincts and your heart. I am only the messenger, and I know no more to tell you. I only know that you have been preparing for this calling all your life."

No matter how she pressed him, the old man could tell her no more; so after the compulsory cup of coffee and some small talk, she rose and left.

She made her way back down the mountain road to San Felipe and managed to book a motel room at the El Cortez, near the beach just south of town. She dropped her bag in her room and headed to the restaurant next to the motel office. The menu was simple—shrimp cocktail, shrimp salad, shrimp dinner, and a good flan for dessert. She had two bottles of fine Mexican beer with her meal. She lingered awhile on the porch overlooking the harbor where there were dozens of shrimp boats moored. Finishing the last of her beer, she headed back to the room and some writing before sleep.

Sometime during the night, Rose became aware of a presence in her room. She was not awake but not

265

asleep and very alert, not a normal sleeping occurrence. A hushed voice came in the darkness calling her name.

"Rosetta … Rose," the voice whispered.

She became awake and sat up in bed. She was alone in the room, but there seemed to be an echo of the whispered voice. Rose got up and check the door and windows, but they were locked. The low hum of the air conditioner was the only sound. Rose went to the bathroom and relieved herself before returning to bed. Once back under the covers, she tossed and turned for what seemed like an eternity before finally succumbing to sleep.

She awakened very slowly. Her head ached like she had a mild hangover, so she attributed her strange experience to the two beers she had with dinner though she had never before had this problem with so little consumption of alcohol. *Maybe one of the shrimp was bad,* she thought though she had no real symptoms of food poisoning, just a slight headache. She pushed it from her mind and got up.

After showering, she packed her bag and tossed it into her dusty Jeep Liberty before heading to the motel office to check out. After a quick breakfast in the motel restaurant, she headed back north for the border. She calculated that she would be home by midafternoon, a 240-mile drive being ahead of her.

Her SUV made easy work of the drive. Though technically a truck, it was comfortable and drove easily. The diesel engine got very good mileage, and she didn't have to stop for fuel, only for relieving herself and pick up some finger food at a convenience store.

Arriving at her little cottage near the university campus, she parked in the attached garage and unloaded the vehicle. It took two trips to drag all her gear into the house. Before unpacking, she checked her refrigerator and found one bottle of Sierra Nevada in the door. She popped the cap and plopped down on her couch to enjoy the cold beer. She could still recall the weird feeling of the previous night, the voice that could have been in her head or an unearthly experience, but she was no closer to understanding what had occurred.

Rather than deplete her meager food stores, Rose elected to drive to the waterfront and have a meal at the City Cafe, known for their fresh seafood. Refreshed from a good meal and glass of wine, Rose returned home and spent two hours organizing her notes from her trip. At last, tired from the long day and drive, she went to bed, intending to finish her writing in the morning. When she awoke, she was naked and lying in the shade of a pinon tree somewhere in the high country.

CAHOKIA

As the summer approached, runners began to return from the search teams bringing news that there more others in other tribal villages. Most of the reports were of stories of spirit world travelers that had arrived in other villages, but a few of them involved actual contact by the team members. Bryan began to compile a list of where the travelers were and their special skills. From the initial reports, it appeared as if the people who came through the Spirit World could make contributions in developing rudimentary technology that could advance the Indian nations to at least a competitive level with fourteenth-century Europe. Runners from the Pawnee village said the reports received by the professor coincided with those that Bryan was hearing.

One of the runners from Many Coups' team brought the message that the Southern Plains Comanche had horses. The runner had no idea what to call them, just that the Comanche were riding speedy animals and were being schooled in equine husbandry by a Spirit World traveler who brought the animals with him.

With no complications or much warning, Strong Woman was delivered of a beautiful baby girl. She had her mother's beauty, and her father's unusual blue eyes. Her raven hair had hints of auburn, and her complexion was a shade between the two of them. Bryan thought his daughter was absolutely flawless. Bryan almost felt neglected as the little girl became the center of attention in his lodge. His joy in his child and his wife's easy delivery prevented Bryan from feeling any neglect; in fact, he reveled in the brief times he was allowed to hold the sleeping child. Bryan was sure that he would be missed somewhat, but he set about planning his departure for Cahokia and beyond.

Accompanied by fourteen warriors, five teams of three, Bryan left the Cheyenne village early in the morning. They settled into a pace-eating dogtrot, and in two days, they were well beyond the hunting grounds of their clan. The ground was mostly open prairie with occasionally ravines or streams that had to be crossed or forded. They took fresh game if the opportunity presented itself, but mostly, they ate jerky or pemmican from their buffalo hide parfleches.

A party of fifteen warriors is small enough to travel fast, but large enough to preclude any hostile attacks, so it was without incident that they crossed the northern high plains and dropped down into the Mississippi Valley. They had made a number of contacts with tribes in small villages along the way and had heard rumors of travelers but had no confirmations.

Near the big river, they encountered a hunting party from the Illinois tribe who invited them to their village. Bryan and his companions accompanied them to a small group of wood covered, framed huts on the banks of a creek that emptied into the Mississippi. Using sign language, they arranged to be transported across the river in the morning. The Illinois chief had heard stories of strangers amongst the peoples to the north and east, but he had not seen any himself. He was fascinated by Bryan's appearance and size and asked if he was Osage, a southern plains Siouxian tribe who were known for being much bigger than normal. He was surprised to learn that he was a spirit traveler.

The Cheyenne group was treated to a fine meal of fresh fish, corn and bean succotash and topped off with a piece of wild honeycomb dripping with sweetness. They opted to sleep around the fire in the central part of the village on sleeping robes provided by the villagers.

In the morning, five canoes were carried to the creek. The Cheyenne and Bryan boarded three to a canoe which each also carried two Illinois paddlers in the bow and stern. The river was past flood stages of the spring, and the crossing was uneventful, except for dodging a few floating trees. After landing their canoes, the Illinois pointed the way south toward Cahokia and Bryan and his group set out.

After a few hours of following a trail along the east bank of the great river, they came to cleared areas that were cultivated. Stalks of what appeared to be corn or maize were showing above the orderly mounds of earth that were in neat, evenly spaced rows. Other fields appeared to contain beans, squash, and other vegetable crops. They saw a few people working in the fields, hoeing and pulling weeds from between the planted mounds. No one seemed surprised to see a group of warriors heading toward Cahokia.

Shortly after midday, Bryan and his teams topped a low rise along the river and saw a sight that stopped them in their tracks. Stretching along a line about a quarter of a mile back from the riverbank was a long mound that appeared to be at least one hundred feet high. It was covered with grass and at the top were trees that had been planted in neat lines. Bryan knew this had to be one of the famous mounds made by the Hopewell people maybe a thousand years before the current time. Just beyond the long mound was a thriving community of what appeared to be wooden houses surrounded by a stockade.

There were a number of well-marked paths leading toward the city from every direction. The one they were on was the closest to the river, but there were at least half a dozen wide, good to travel roads coming into the city from other points on the compass.

Bryan and his team discussed their approach. Bryan took charge and said that they would enter the city and locate the chief or chiefs and tell them of their quest. With no more talk, they took up the trail again; and shortly, they were jogging up to a broad, open gate in the stockade.

As the path began to converge with other pathways into the city, they encountered other groups of people heading in the same direction, most of whom were carrying large packs on their backs or bundles of furs slung on a pole between two men. Other than a few cursory stares, the Cheyenne group was pretty much ignored until they arrived at the gates. A small group of well-armed warriors was checking the travelers as they entered the enclosed city. Bryan and his group were motioned aside.

The leader of the gate guards signed, "Who are you, and what is your business in our city?"

"We wish to speak with your chief," signed Bryan displaying the wampum belt of his clan. "We are seekers of Spirit World travelers, and we have heard that there may be knowledge of them here. We have come from The People who live on the Great Plains, The Cheyenne."

"We have many chiefs here, but our civil leader may be able to help. Gray Wolf here will take you," signed the guard leader, indicating a dark visaged brave.

Bryan and his group followed Gray Wolf into the city and down a broad main street toward the center of the town. Shortly, they entered a large open area, sort of like a village square. There was a market set up in the square and lively trading was going on. To Bryan, it looked like what he imagined a Middle Ages English Market would be like. There were individual areas with wares displayed. There were booths with pottery, some with woven blankets, and others with tools of knapped flint.

Bryan was about to pass one display and suddenly realized he was looking at metal tools, arrow, and spearheads, tomahawks, and pots and pans. He called the others to a halt, and they began to examine the amazing wares. A large, well-made man in buckskins noticed their attention and came over to them. Bryan was startled as was the trader when they realized they were each looking at another white man.

Big Larry Stamps had been working for months at his smithy. He had developed a great skill in fashioning weapons, tools, and cooking vessels for his tribe, and then he had made a large batch to be taken to a trading village to the southeast of their home on the Great Lake.

A great trading trip was planned, and Larry was to be accompanied by a dozen or more men who were also taking wares to be traded. Their destination was a week's travel away, and from what Larry could understand, it was a center for Indian trading from all tribes for hundreds of miles in every direction.

Larry seemed to recall from his reading about Native America that the Indian people were great traders, and there were established trade routes in many parts of the country. Most of the tribes realized that there was more to be gained by commerce than by war, a facet of Indian life that wasn't taught when Big Larry was in school. In Mexico, Central and South America, there were trade routes between all the population centers and goods from the Incas often found their way into what is now the United States. The Incas, Mayan, Toltec, and Aztecs had invented looms and wove fabrics from wool and cotton, the latter a plant indigenous to their part of the world.

The Indians of the Americas had also developed some metalworking skills, mostly in soft metals like gold that appeared in a nearly refined state naturally. They also worked raw copper and iron found in the remnants of meteorites that hit the earth.

Larry now found himself trudging along a trail south of the Great Lake following the lead warrior in the group. They had used two of their big open-water canoes to transport their bundles as far as they could in the lake and up one of the rivers that flowed in from the southeast. When they had paddled as far as they could, they disembarked and unloaded their packs. Four warriors were left to take the big canoes back out to the lake and across to their village. They would return in two weeks to pick up the traders.

That night, the traders and Larry arrived at another village of their people. It was located on a small river that flowed to the south away from a small lake. Larry and the leader of the traders bargained with the local people for the use of four of their smaller canoes. The canoe owners were so taken with Big Larry's iron tomahawk head, spear points, and arrowheads that the traders got a bargain. The next morning, they launched on what would be a three-day trip down the river, which grew increasingly larger until Larry was sure that it was the Mississippi.

The Ojibwa traders arrived at Cahokia and entered the city. They sought out the man overseeing the marketplace and made arrangements for space for their wares. It cost them a few furs, a block of pemmican, and one of Larry's axe heads.

The set up their booth, and most of the Ojibwa traders began to check out the items in the other booths. Larry was going to do the same when he noticed a group of strangely clad warriors had stopped to look at his iron implements. He approached them and found himself looking into the eyes of another white man.

CHANGING HISTORY

Charles Branson, the professor, had been receiving the reports of all of the Pawnee teams of seekers and now with Bryan on a trek, he was getting runners from the Cheyenne camp as well. Most of the runners had made contact with tribes who either knew of a Spirit World traveler or had one in their village. The reports indicated a vast variety of skills represented by the spirit travelers.

From the southwest (present-day Texas), he learned that the Comanche people on the Staked Plains had been brought a breeding herd of horses, accompanied by a knowledgeable horseman. The Chumash from the West Coast had a linguist proficient in indigenous languages, most notably the Indian tongues of the Southwest and Northern Mexico. There were reports of shipbuilders, sailing captains, specialists in animal husbandry, and a host of other trades and professions. The picture the professor was getting was that the gathering of the Spirit World travelers possessed all the technology to rapidly bring the New World up to the same level as Europe, maybe even higher, since many of the "baby steps" could be eliminated.

His calculations indicated that they had at the most 150 years for the Americas to be prepared for the coming invasion from Europe.

It may be enough time, he thought. *I wonder what happens to us when we have them started on the right path? I hope I just stay here for the rest of my days.*

The professor put his fine mind to the problem of how to bring together all the diverse cultures, languages, and cultures into one united people.

'I guess this is what the founders of the American republic felt,' he reflected. *'They were faced with much the same situation, except they already had a hostile presence in the form of the English overlords of the colonies'.*

He thought further that they should centralize the technology and cross teach both the spirit travelers and the Native Americans the basics. There were some giant steps to be taken, first to gain the acceptance of the Indian tribes, then to establish schools, factories, shipyards, foundries, textile mills, farms, ranches, orchards... There would be resistance, of course, but there would be core of smart, young people who would be readily trained. In turn, their children would be more accepting, and by the next generation, there would be widespread improvement in the knowledge and technology.

What about the spirit warriors, those who had traveled through the spirit world to this time and place? he thought. My guess is that they will remain here permanently... "I certainly hope so." He said the last aloud. *Bryan will*

use his channel through Charlie Littlebear to send messages back to friends and relatives who may be concerned about the disappearance of these folks. We have to be sure that there is closure for everyone...

"*Yes,*" thought Branson, "*We will have enough time, but we have to get to work fast. Some of the issues we have to prepare these people for are the worst that the Europeans bring with them: diseases bred in the filth and poor hygiene of European cities, slavery that was universal, even here in the Americas, avarice, cruelty, and oppressive regimes. The Americas were not without these latter flaws, but only among the developed peoples of Mexico and South America were they as advanced as in the Old World.*"

He reflected on the history of his time, how the great horse culture of the American plains evolved in less than three hundred years. Beginning with a few stolen or escaped horses, the Indians were soon mounted for traveling, hunting, and fighting, first on the southern plains but spreading north up into Canada. Some tribes, like the Nez Perce of the Pacific Northwest, became accomplished horse breeders, but all of them developed great horse herds and this changed their lifestyles completely.

The bison were the primary source of nearly everything in the nomadic plains tribal life: food, clothing, shelter, utensils, ornaments, costumes, bedding, glue, needles, and other tools. Every aspect of Plains Indian lives involved the bison. With the horse, they no longer had to wait for the buffalo to migrate into their area, but they could now search for these beasts that represented their prosperity.

The professor, Bryan, and the others had a huge advantage. They knew what the history of their country was, and they had the skills to try to change that history which was the future of the people in this time and place.

EPILOGUE

Jaboa stood behind the helmsman and surveyed the deckhands' activity following his order for more sail. He gazed aloft and watched two seamen loose another sheet into the wind from their precarious perch on the yardarms. The sail billowed and caught the stiff breeze quartering from the starboard and the small caravel heeled a bit from the added pressure. The helmsman spun the wheel clockwise to counteract the push of the wind, maintaining their westerly course.

They were en route from their home port in Malaga to this "India" discovered by that fool Italian, Christobal Colon. Jaboa had orders from the grand admiral to go quickly before the Italian had organized his return to the discovered land. He was to reconnoiter and report back to the admiralty. The political ramifications of the influence Colon had with the queen disturbed the military and civil hierarchy, and they wanted to be sure of an accurate accounting of the Italian's find.

They were more than a month into their journey, having dropped south along the coast of Africa to pick up the easterlies. Once the trade winds had filled their sails, they moved briskly to the west. Emboldened by Colon's successful return, Jaboa and his men, all experienced seamen, were excited about their voyage of exploration, this feeling continuing even though they had been at sea for thirty-six days now. They still had enough food and fresh water for several more weeks though they were out of citrus fruit, their safeguard against that dreaded disease, scurvy.

Jaboa watched as the pilot marked their speed, dropping the small piece of wood overboard at the rail marking near the bow, beginning his chant as he followed the bobbing missile along the rail. When it passed the second mark, the chant ceased, the syllable where it stopped indicated the speed as shown on the mnemonic. The pilot marked the speed on the traverse board, noting that they were maintaining a pace of more one Spanish league per hour since picking up the trade winds.

Masters, pilot-navigators, and ships officers were trained in the dead-reckoning method of navigation in this year of 1493. Jaboa, a Portuguese by birth, had recently become familiar with his kinsmen's use of the stars for navigation. He had acquired the tools used by them and had studied their use. He had been using both methods since leaving port and found celestial navigation far more accurate. He kept his quadrant and nocturnal in his master's cabin under lock and key, but the sandglass and compass were mounted near the ship's tiller with another compass on the quarterdeck for use by the officer of the deck. The sandglass was turned hourly by the cabin boy or a deckhand assigned to the duty. Jaboa used the nocturnal to calculate true midnight from which the glass was started each day. His master's log kept track of the daily progress which was measured in leagues, roughly four miles, if using the Spanish measurement, 3.2 miles for the Italian. With two navigational methods employed, his recording of their voyage was quite accurate.

Jaboa had attended Colon's audience with the admiralty and heard the Italian describe the islands of his landfall and the indigenous peoples he found there—dark of skin and hair, much like the people of India were reported to be, but quite primitive in their lodgings, watercraft, and lifestyle. Colon believed that mainland India lay not too far to the west of the tropical islands he discovered. He had not expanded his exploration other than a cruise past the other nearby isles, several of which were quite large, requiring several days to sail around. After repairing and restocking his ships and resting the crew, Colon had returned to Spain to report his findings and make preparations to return to the New World with more ships, men and equipment to colonize and explore.

The grand admiral, wanting to assure the control by the admiralty of Colon's finds, convened a meeting of his staff who recommended a fast ship and loyal crew be dispatched to verify the findings and then search farther to the West for the mainland. The orders were to make contact with the native peoples and make a determination as to what valuable cargo could be brought back to Spain to provide a much needed financial boost for the nearly bankrupt nation. The admiral hoped that his swift and decisive actions would allow him to appoint his choices for the governor and staff to administer to these new lands.

Jaboa, one of their most competent navigators, was put in charge of the expedition that consisted of one swift caravel and a crew of forty, twenty-five sailors and a squad of lightly armored infantry soldiers with their signature steel helmets.

The lookout above called out a sighting off the port bow. Jaboa moved to the rail and saw what caused the shout. A flock of seabirds was wheeling above a large patch of floating seaweed, which must harbor some of the small fish the birds preyed upon. It was a good sign, an indication that land was not far off.

Sure enough, shortly after midday, a dark line appeared on the western horizon. The lookout called out the sighting of land ahead. The caravel drew closer over the next few hours, and the landmass began to assume shape and details became evident. It was apparently a heavily forested island or maybe a cape extending from a mainland still too distant to see. Just before nightfall, the caravel had drawn close to the shore, and they turned northward, hunting a safe haven in which to anchor. A small bay was sighted, and soon, the sails were furled and the anchor was dropped. There was nothing but quiet after the splash of the anchor. The crew looked to the tree-lined shore but saw nothing more than the vegetation out of which sprouted tall palm trees, their trunks festooned with dead fronds lying tightly against their boles, except for the display of green at their tops.

Jaboa elected to wait until first light before sending a party to the shore to reconnoiter. Their first task would be to locate fresh water to replenish the ship's casks. He intended to sail along the coastline until he made contact with native peoples or located a more suitable harbor, then explore further. The land appeared much as described by the Italian, tropical greenery growing nearly to the waters edge bordered by a narrow strip of white sandy beach. To celebrate their successful arrival in the New World, Jaboa ordered a cask of wine be broached and for the cook to prepare the best meal possible from their limited stores.

The early morning showed promise of being a nice day. There were only wisps of clouds on the eastern horizon, and the sky glowed yellow heralding the imminent arrival of the sun. The night had passed quietly and had been warm so many of the sailors had slept on deck. The shore party assembled by the rail as the skiff was launched. The rope boarding net was hung over the side and several of the men clambered down into the skiff. Empty water kegs were handed down and the rest of the shore party descended into the skiff. The oarsmen pulled strongly away from the caravel and headed through the light surf to the beach. The skiff was pulled out, and the party, made up of five soldiers and their officer and four oarsmen, marched in loose formation down the beach, looking for a pathway into the forest. Jaboa watched from the high stern of the ship as they veered into the trees and disappeared from view.

The remainder of the crew busied themselves with repairing gear, patching sails and other tasks that befall a seaman after a long ocean voyage. Jaboa updated the ship's log and made notes of their passage in his journal.

Shortly before noon, the shore party returned. From the way they lugged the casks, it was apparent they had found fresh water. Jaboa had to suppress the desire to rush to the rail to greet the returning officer, waiting instead on the high stern castle of the ship for his report.

The young officer reported that they had found a stream of fresh water that flowed from the mountain to the west. There were no signs of animals, but a number of birds were seen, most numerous of which were large flocks of colorful parrots. The water they bore in casks was emptied into the water barrels and the water carriers returned to the stream for more. After several trips all the water supplies had been replenished.

Jaboa ordered the anchors raised and sail hoisted, intending to explore along the coast to the north. The ship moved through the channel and heeled to the port as the easterly filled the sails. As they made their way, several lookouts were posted aloft to look for signs of habitation.

In late afternoon, they spotted a small native village in a cove. The houses were on stilts and had thatched roofs and sides and appeared to be arranged along a short street or village square. There were several dugout canoes pulled up on the beach and a number of people grouped at the entrance to the village as if awaiting the arrival of the Spanish ship. Jaboa figured that they had been spotted quite a while before by native scouts, but he was puzzled that there didn't seem to be any alarm on the part of the villagers.

The ship hove to and an anchor was dropped as the sails were furled. Jaboa ordered a skiff launched and a shore party formed, consisting of a four sailors, a half squad of soldiers, their officer, and himself. The sailors pulled at their oars and beached the boat smartly near the native canoes. After they pulled it up further, the soldiers disembarked and formed up. Jaboa stepped to the sand and proceeded to the village at the head of the squad. He knew that they must make an impressive sight, with the colorful tunics, steel helmets, and long lances. He was wearing his sword but no steel helmet. Rather he had opted for a large-brimmed hat with a sweeping ostrich feather.

As they approached the villagers, he could see that there seemed to be a central group of dignitaries surrounded by young men, none of whom were armed. The people were of moderate height, dark skinned but only a shade darker than some of the Spaniards or Portuguese in the crew. Their black hair was cropped off in a circle around their heads almost as if it had been trimmed around the edge of a bowl. Their features were regular and finely made. The young men were wearing woven loin cloths, while the older men were also clothed in short woven shawls over their shoulders.

Jaboa drew to a halt a few yards from the natives. At a command from the officer, the soldiers moved smartly from their column of twos into two ranks behind the navigator. Jaboa raised his hand, palm outward, in the universal sign of peace. One of the older men moved forward a few steps and responded in kind while uttering what Jaboa took to be words of welcome in his native tongue. Then to Jaboa's surprise, he said in passable Spanish, "Welcome to our village. Please enter in peace. We have been expecting you."

The old man turned and headed toward the village. Jaboa moved after him, and the soldiers once again formed into a column of twos. The other villagers fell in around them, but not so close as to cause alarm. The sailors remained with the skiff.

Later in the evening, after the explorers had returned to their ship, Jaboa lay awake in his bunk, reflecting on what had happened in the village. The Spaniards had been feted with a feast of native foods, some of which were recognizable like pork in various styles—roasted, stewed and broiled but also cooked in a pit lined with hot stones. This "bar-ba-quoa" was juicy and delicious. After the meal, they were served a surprisingly good native beer.

In response to his many questions, Jaboa was advised by the elder village leader that the answers lay several days journey to the northwest, on the mainland. The elder was polite but firm in his refusal to provide answers, only saying that Jaboa and his crew were expected as was the expedition of the Italian, Colon, though the latter had only made contact with people on the outer islands and thus had not received the welcoming message to proceed to the mainland.

On the morrow, after restocking his vessel with fresh fruits, vegetables, and live meats in the form of fowl and pigs, provided by the willing villagers, anchor was hoisted, sails loosened, and the caravel sailed toward the northwest.

On the third day, the lookout sighted sails off their port stern quarter. As it neared, they were amazed to see a sleek sailing ship of three square rigged masts traveling on a parallel course. This vessel lacked the high stern castle of the Spanish and Portuguese style but rather had a lower profile and was moving at much greater speed than the caravel could ever achieve. The vessel passed them quickly without slowing or any recognition other than a wave from the watch officer standing by the helmsman. Several crew members, attired in white, were aloft in the rigging. The stunned navigator watched as the vessel pulled away, leaving the caravel in its wake. While the clipper's sails were still barely visible on the horizon, the lookout called out the sighting of land dead ahead.

Three hours later, the caravel passed around the southern tip of a long barrier island and entered a bay or sound. There were scattered houses on both sides of the waterway that grew more numerous as the ship neared what appeared to be a large harbor on the mainland side. They entered the harbor and Jaboa was amazed to see many sailing vessels similar to the one that had flown past them earlier. There were wharfs and quays on which there was a bustle of commercial activity—loading and unloading of cargo.

The sails were furled, and the caravel slowed to a halt as the anchors were dropped in the common mooring area. Almost immediately, a large barge with banks of rowers and filled with uniformed men put out from shore. When the barge drew alongside, the apparent leader asked in passable Spanish for permission to come aboard. Jaboa immediately granted the request.

The uniformed officers boarded the Spanish ship and correctly saluted to standard at the stern and the navigator. The leader extended his hand and said, "Welcome to our land. We invite you come ashore and discuss your mission with our council of leaders. But first, there will be a banquet in your honor. We have been preparing a long time for your visit as foretold by our seers."

Jaboa and his four officers accompanied the greeting committee in the barge. Their crew would be left aboard but supplied with a meal by the banquet chefs.

The Portuguese and his Spanish officers were amazed at the city they entered. The streets were clean and well paved with some sort of black surfactant. Horse-drawn wagons and carriages abounded, and the people were dressed in well-tailored clothing of loomed fabrics. The clothing style was far different from the foppish wear of the European upper classes and rather more casual in appearance. The people themselves were tall, well-formed with dusky complexions and dark hair worn in a variety of styles. The houses were sited on spacious lots and were painted in subdued hues, much in the style of the Dutch cities.

The visiting officer was taken to what appeared to be a government building formed from blocks of stone. A representative of the council of leaders met them on the landing and conducted them into a sizable hall where a group of men and women were waiting their arrival.

Jaboa was surprised to see women amongst the council members, but he was even more surprised to see several men who looked like African natives to him. In all, the council was about twenty people of various ages but mostly of middle years.

The spokesperson for the council stepped forward and greeted the Portuguese navigator. "Welcome to our city. We wish to open trading agreements with Spain and other European countries, and we have awaited your first visit with great anticipation. Tonight, we will celebrate your visit with a feast, and tomorrow we will show you some of what we have to offer." The spokesman went on, "We know that you and your men are explorers not the national leaders, so we will send back a message with you to your rulers after you have seen our capabilities."

The banquet that night was a repeat of the one in the village, though on a much larger scale. There was a whole roasted cow on a spit, pork cooked in a variety of ways, fowl and fish of every variety imaginable. The vegetables were unlike any Jaboa and his men had ever seen. There were ears of corn, tubers, squash of several types, beans, and fiery red chillies in a delicious but spicy sauce. The beer and wines were very good.

On the next morning, after a hearty breakfast at the inn where they were quartered, the visiting officers were given a tour of the city, the industrial areas, and in particular, of the defenses. Jaboa was amazed to see how sophisticated their cannons were. Instead of muzzle-loading pieces, these were breech-loaded with a metallic cartridge bearing a pointed projectile. A demonstration of the efficiency of these canon left Jaboa and his officers knowing that nothing Spain could mount would overcome the range and effectiveness of these weapons. They could see that this city was defended by hundreds of these field pieces.

At the shipyard, Jaboa saw the sharp bow and keel of a vessel pulled for a bottom cleaning. The yard was large and efficient as evidenced by the number of ships under construction and in dry-docks for servicing.

After several days of viewing the capability of these "Indians," the Spanish officers were humbled.

On their last day before setting sail for Spain, Jaboa and the officers met with the council again. A formal proposal had been prepared for the king and queen and sealed in a tight metal box. Gifts of gold and silver were also boxed. Jaboa was briefed on the trade agreement: The Spanish were allowed to visit these lands but could only settle here with permission of the ruling body. They would have to adhere to the laws of this land if they wanted to trade or become residents. The laws prohibited slavery or oppression of any group, but equally, the Spanish would be similarly protected. The Spanish would benefit greatly from the trading agreement, which covered all the lands of this western hemisphere, but any attempts at conquest would be met with great force.

"You have seen our capability, so please impart your observations to your leaders so that they will know that we could easily prevent Spain from entering our lands and could make a deal with England, France, or the Dutch. In fact, we intend to meet with these countries and others to offer similar agreements, but they will be consigned to other areas of our vast lands. Our united states have lands that exceed all of those of European countries several times over, so there is room for all to do business or settle."

Jaboa sailed the next morning with the first tide. He was bearing a message for the king and queen, not the one they expected to hear, but it was still one of hope for their depleted treasury. The goods of Spain would be paid for in gold. They would also be provided with plants and animals that would thrive in Spain and contribute to the prosperity of the people. And they would be welcome to settle in some areas of this new and great land. No conquest, but the chance to contribute to this great land and to benefit from unlimited opportunity. Jaboa was thinking that he might just return to settle here with his family.